THE HORSE TRADER

Also by Lynn Hall

THE LEAVING

THE HORSE TRADER

❧ Lynn Hall ❧

CHARLES SCRIBNER'S SONS | NEW YORK

Copyright © 1981 Lynn Hall

Library of Congress Cataloging in Publication Data
Hall, Lynn.   The horse trader.
SUMMARY: A fatherless teenage girl's special
friendship with Harley Williams, the local horse
trader and con man, begins to change after she buys
one of his horses.
[1.   Horses—Fiction]   I.   Title.
PZ7.H1458Hq   [Fic]   80-26533
ISBN 0-684-16852-9

3 5 7 9 11 13 15 17 19 F/C 20 18 16 14 12 10 8 6 4

Printed in the United States of America

❧ One ❧

On a barren stretch of Highway 6 near Palisade, Nebraska, a red stock truck roared steadily west, reflecting sunset from its windshield. Above the cab, the stock box carried a homemade sign that said, "Here Comes Harley."

Here came Harley, indeed. He was a big man, a vital man, weathering well through his fifties. A cream Stetson temporarily hid silver curls. His eyes were requisite cowboy eyes, small and deep-set and pale blue. The features in the leathery red face were large and good, full lips and a cleft chin, and a super-abundance of impressive white teeth.

He drove with his arm out the window, fist braced against the side mirror, his shirt sleeve billowing in the wind. His denim-clad legs were bowed, as though

1

they had been formed by a horse's barrel. His bronze belt buckle was fashioned in the shape of a bronco.

At a shabby roadside cafe-motel he slowed the truck to a gentle stop, conscious of the ten horses in the box behind him. He got out, stretched mightily, took a quick check of the horses to be sure none was in trouble back there. The horses were packed so closely together that falling would have been nearly impossible. They stood crossways in the truck, north-south, north-south, their halter ropes tied to the planks of the stock box.

He went inside and took a booth by the front window. The cafe was almost deserted. At one of the three tables a family of tourists were finishing their suppers accompanied by the noisy restlessness of children confined to the car all day.

Harley stretched again, rubbed the hard muscles of his stomach, enjoyed his hunger. A little supper, couple more hours on the road, unload the horses, check in with Gloria, then maybe a drink or two at Max's if he felt like it.

He gave the waitress his finest grin and said, "Howdy there, how you tonight? I believe I'll just have a nice big hamburger, bowl of chili, big plate of onion rings'd be nice. Coffee."

His smile remained after the departing waitress; it was there for anyone who wanted to pick up on it. One of the children at the center table had turned away from his empty plate and met Harley's smile by accident. He smiled back. He was a narrow, nicely dressed boy of about twelve or thirteen.

"That your truck out there?" the boy asked, nodding toward the window.

"Sure is."

"Got horses in it, don't you?"

"Yep. Ten of 'em."

"Ten horses, all yours?" The boy's eyes widened and Harley felt a glow, an expanding in his chest. When his chili arrived he managed to inhale it without losing the boy's attention.

"Oh, those ten aren't much, compared to what's at home. I just needed a few more head, to fill out my cowpony string."

The boy slipped into Harley's booth and leaned toward the man. His parents were deep in conference over their road map.

"Have you got a *ranch*?"

Harley's smile widened again, and he gave a modest nod. "Where you folks from?" he asked, secure in the knowledge that he would soon again be the focus of the conversation.

"Minneapolis. We're on our vacation. We're going to the Rocky Mountains. Is that where you live?"

Harley received his burger and onion rings. "No, my spread is just this side of the mountains. The mountains are purty, but the flatlands, that's where the real cattle country is. The big spreads."

"Is that what you got? Like on television? With roundups and doggies and all that?"

3

Harley shrugged with admirable modesty. "Somethin' like that."

"Do you own it all?" The boy's face was glowing, and Harley basked in his adulation. "Is it fancy?"

"Nah," Harley laughed. "I wouldn't call it fancy. It's comfortable, though. Got a nice log house, stone fireplaces, that sort of thing. A few moose antlers here and there, couple of bearskin rugs with the heads left on 'em. Chun Lo, that's my cook, he's always tripping over them rugs, and cussing me out in Chinese. Here, have an onion ring."

They munched in companionable silence, and the boy gazed again through the window at the truck outside.

His mother said, "Matt, are you eating that man's dinner, for heaven's sake? If you're still hungry come back here and finish your own food, don't go bothering strangers."

Harley beamed his smile across the room to the woman and saw her melt. "He's not a bit of bother, ma'am. We're just having a visit here."

"Well," the woman said, subsiding, "if you get tired of him, you send him on back."

Matt turned away from the window and said, "Are those broncos out there?" He took another onion ring.

"They're unbroke young stock," Harley explained. "I just bought 'em in Saint Jo, and I'll take 'em home and break 'em, and in a few weeks they'll be good little working cowponies."

4

"You break them yourself?" The boy's face was alight.

"Me and a few of my hands. Well, sir, it's been a pleasure visiting with you." Harley stood and fished three dollars from his tooled cowhide wallet. "You have a good trip now, hear?"

With a wink for the boy and one for the mother, Harley left the cafe.

The sun was at the horizon now, and comfortably dimmed. Harley aimed the red truck straight toward it, humming along with the country-western radio music, and occasionally belching onion and chili. He felt good, nourished by the meal and the boy's admiration.

Nice little bugger. I expect that'll be a real memory for the boy, meeting a rancher and getting to visit like that. He's going to go home to Minneapolis and tell all his friends about it, play big shot with them. He'll get a kick out of that.

His thoughts grew vague as they followed the song lyrics for a few minutes, then turned to the horses in the truck behind him. *A good trip, this time. Full load, and there should be a margin on all of them. Let's see, the buckskin gelding at two-fifty, that was the highest I had to pay for any of them, but he's going to bring five, no problem there. Any kind of a buckskin is going to bring a good price, and he's a nice-looking animal. The two palominos, same thing. Not a very pretty color, either of them, too washed-out, but a palomino's always going to sell. Nice little spotted*

5

pony, won't bring much, but he didn't cost much. The others, let's see, that little bay looked quick. Can probably pass him off as a gaming pony. Barrel racer. Brown mare for the little Kohler girl, maybe.

In the deepening night the Colorado state line passed by unnoticed. Houses along the highway were rare, and towns even more so. But the road, devoid as it was of landmarks, was familiar enough to Harley that he began to feel home up ahead.

The little Kohler girl. Karen. Not so little anymore. Must be up in her teens now. Is that possible? I can't be getting that old surely. Why, I was, what, in my thirties when Karen's mama was hanging around the shows and rodeos in those tight pants, tight shirts. I used to wonder how she ever got up on that crushin' big palomino of hers without ripping the seams right out of those pants. She was a little firecracker all right, that Della. Liked the men. Me, especially.

His face softened with the memory.

I believe she was in love with me, yes sir. Believe she was. Couldn't have me, so she run off and got herself pregnant, just to spite me. If it wasn't for me being a gentleman, Karen might have never got born. He smiled and shook his head. *Life's a puzzle, that's for sure. Here's that baby girl all grown up, and I'm not a day older than I was before she was born.*

"There she is," he said aloud, as the lights of Sand Hills appeared in the velvet black landscape. He drove through the little town, waving at the few people he passed, then turned south on the old blacktop and drove out into the country again, more slowly now because of the road's cracks and potholes. Three miles out, he turned onto a narrow, rutted track. A weather-beaten plank over the track said "Harley Williams, Horses Bought and Sold," and crude horse heads burned into the wood on either end.

There were two buildings, a house, small and bare and justifiably deserted, and a barn that stood stark and swaybacked against the starry sky. Next to the barn was a pole corral and a loading chute, into which Harley expertly backed the truck.

With admirable economy of motion Harley removed the tailgate, untied each of the ten horses and turned them loose in the corral after a clattering trip down the loading chute. He turned on the switch at the water tank and let it fill; then, with only a brief glance at his new purchases, Harley replaced the tailgate and drove down the rutted lane, onto the somewhat smoother blacktop, and headed for home.

The business district of Sand Hills was two blocks long. Past the first block, Harley turned onto a side street, then turned again into the alley behind the block of stores. His parking space was behind Gloria's beauty shop, but the truck crowded over into the area behind the shoe store because it was so big. The area was littered with stacks of cartons to be hauled away, small ones from the shoe store and huge ones from the hardware store beyond it. The clutter was familiar, even pleasant to Harley. It was home.

He climbed the open wooden stairway behind the

beauty shop and let himself in. The kitchen was dark but he found his way easily past the table and the portable dishwasher, for which they hadn't yet found adequate space in the cramped room.

"I'm home, honey."

"So am I, but not yelling about it." Gloria's voice came from the living room at the front of the apartment. She looked up from the television set as Harley came into the room. She didn't turn down the volume, but raised her voice to a level of successful competition with it.

"You have a good trip?"

"Purty good, purty good. How's things here?"

"Same."

He aimed a kiss in the general direction of the top of her head, and she gave him a pat on the back that was almost a hug. She was a tall, thin woman with unbelievably bright gold hair and false eyelashes, the only pair in Sand Hills. She enjoyed experimenting on herself with all of the new cosmetics and hair tints that came into the shop, but she had no illusions about her fifty-year-old face and hands. No matter. Her hair was as young as Max Factor could make it, and her fingernails were plum purple, and she was having a good time with this life of hers. The shop supported her and Harley, and provided her with women to talk to all day, and when she wanted loving Harley was usually around and willing. The bills got paid and the TV got good reception, and she was content.

Harley looked at the television screen for a minute, picking up on the story. Then he stared thoughtfully at Gloria's beer can, on the coffee table beside her.

"Want one?" Gloria asked. "There's plenty in the fridge. Want a sandwich or something?"

"No sandwich, thanks. I might have a beer, though. Unless you want to go down to the bar with me for a while. Sit around and tip a few?"

"I don't think so," Gloria said. "You go if you want. I want to see the end of this program. It's pretty good."

Harley weighed the pleasure of going to the bar against the bother of walking the half block to get there, and decided not to bother. He got a can of beer from the kitchen, then paused beside the phone. The kitchen clock said nine-thirty. Not too late to call that little Kohler girl. He picked up the tiny Sand Hills phone directory and looked up Kohler, Della. As he dialed, Harley thought about the brown mare, what she had and what she needed. He thought about her background, her life back there in Missouri; he marshaled his facts.

✖ Two ✖

Five blocks away, on a dusty side street at the edge of town, stood a twelve-year-old mobile home, turquoise and white, with a varnished pine room built onto the side. The lawn was mostly sand, but it was enclosed by a neat miniature picket fence, and shaded by a huge old cottonwood. Della's rusted Pinto stood nose to nose with the trailer, and Karen's bike leaned against the trash-can rack nearby. The Colorado sky, brilliant with stars, formed a dramatic and complimentary backdrop, lending a nonexistent dignity to the dwelling.

Karen sat on the front steps breaking twigs and tossing them at the side of the trailer. She was small for fifteen, and her face had a childlike quality that would remain most of her life. Her hair was raggedly chopped because she insisted on cutting it herself, and her eyes were large and fine. The eyes, the hair, the bony little body gave her a waiflike air that was in part genuine and in part at odds with a developing intellect, a thin but sturdy core of self-reliance.

Tonight her aching impatience was too large to be contained in the cramped rooms of the trailer. Outdoors was better, although the bumps in the iron stairs hurt her fanny, and the wrought-iron railing dug into her spine.

A light was shining in the window beside the steps. Karen turned toward it and said, "Why can't I just go and see if his truck is back yet?"

She heard her mother rustling the pages of her insurance textbook. The rustling was loud and deliberate. "Don't interrupt my studying," it said.

"Because I said you can't. You're not going to go wandering around alleys this time of night looking for Harley Williams, and you are most certainly *not* going in any taverns looking for him. I'm sure he'll let you know if and when he has a horse for you to look at."

"I won't go *in* the tavern. I could just stick my head in and see if he's there."

"That's no place for any part of you, even your head."

"You go there," Karen argued, knowing it was hopeless.

"I'm over twenty-one, cupcake. Now will you please shut up and let me concentrate? I'm trying to understand annuities, and it's complicated."

Karen sank back into daydreams of her horse, and

Harley. She brought out one of her best memories and replayed it behind closed eyes. She had biked out to Harley's barn early that spring, to let him know that her horse fund was over the hundred-fifty-dollar mark, and to see if he had a horse he'd sell her for that amount.

He had stood like a giant against the sky, his face shadowed by his hat, so that only his toothy grin was visible. He had stroked back her hair, cupping his big hand behind her head, and said in his beautiful soft voice, "Don't you worry, honey. Old Harley is going to find just the right horse for you. You don't want any of these that I got now. Half of 'em ain't even broke good, and the others'd be too rough for you. But I travel all over this part of the country, and I'll be on the lookout for a nice little mare for you, one that's broke the best. You're a precious little gal, you know. We don't want you getting busted up on some ole bronc."

Karen remembered every word. She knew his response by heart.

She heard her mother standing in the door behind her. Della said, "Why are you so antsy tonight? You don't even know when he's supposed to get—"

The phone shrilled.

Karen rushed past her mother and grabbed it. "Hello," she said breathlessly.

"Hi Karen, this is Harley."

She sank back against the wall in a wash of relief, then stiffened. "Did you find a horse for me?"

"Well now"—the smile was rich in his voice—"I've got a little bay mare that I think you might like. She's about the size you wanted, and she's broke the best."

Karen screeched. She couldn't help herself. Then she settled down and said, "Tell me everything about her. How soon can I come and see her?"

"Do you think you can stand to wait till morning?"

Karen laughed. "I doubt it, but I'll try."

"What say if I come by and pick you up, about nine. You can ride out with me, if you don't mind hanging around while I do some work out there. I'll tell you all about the mare then, okay?"

"Nine o'clock. I'll be waiting."

Karen hung up and turned to her mother with shining eyes. "He got my horse! A fourteen-hand bay mare, 'broke the best,' he said. I'm going to go out to his place with him in the morning, and see her. Oh, I'm so excited. I'll have to get my money out of the bank. They don't open till nine, though, do they? How can I work that? Let's see—"

"Whoa, Nellybelle," Della said. Her expression was an equal balance of pleasure and caution. "Don't go making any decision till after you've seen the horse. You want to be sure the mare is sound and healthy, and you want to try her out, be sure she's gentle and doesn't have any vices. I've known Harley a good deal longer than you have, and I wouldn't—"

Karen flared, "Don't you dare say anything against Harley. He's my friend. He likes me, and he wants me to have a good horse. Look how long it's taken him

13

to find one that he thought was right for me. He wouldn't try to sell me one that wasn't right."

"I didn't mean—I only meant that horse trading is his business"—Della's voice rose to follow Karen as the girl dove for the shelter of her own room and shut the door—"he's in it to make a profit, and I just want you to be a little careful, that's all. I don't want you getting hurt."

Karen didn't answer, and a heavy stillness descended on the trailer. She turned on her radio to break the silence, then sprawled out on the bed to lose herself in visions of a lovely, dainty, bright bay mare. Her coat would be a rich red, contrasting with her black mane and tail and socks and ear rims. She'd have maybe one white foot, and a neat little star, perhaps a narrow blaze. Her head would be a little bit Arabian, and there'd be a nice arch to her neck. And she'd recognize Karen as her new master, right away. She'd nuzzle her neck, blow on her hair.

Like a wraparound projection screen, the walls of Karen's room reflected her mental images. Two large posters dominated one wall, stallions galloping against a stormy sky, and a mare and foal in a flowery meadow. Smaller pictures covered much of the remaining wall space, some cut from horse magazines and several drawn by Karen herself. The drawings were quite good. A herd of plastic horses lived on the dresser, fighting for space with underwear and notebooks.

Far to the rear of the dresser top, behind the clutter,

stood a newspaper photograph in a cardboard frame. It showed Della Kohler astride an impressive palomino in silver-mounted parade tack. Della at seventeen looked very much as she looked now, except that the girl in the picture wore her tan curls in a shoulder-length mass under her cowgirl hat. In her arms she held a bouquet of long-stemmed roses, and her face radiated triumph. A banner across her chest and half-hidden by the roses, said, "Cheyenne Rodeo Queen."

Karen kept the picture on her dresser because she didn't want to hurt her mother by putting it in a drawer. But she managed to keep it hidden behind piles of clutter, so she didn't have to look at it, didn't have to be reminded—

A light knock jarred Karen from her thoughts. Della's voice said, through the door, "Can I come in a minute? I've got a peace offering."

Something to eat, I bet, Karen thought. She sat up. "Sure. Come on in."

But it wasn't food in Della's hand. It was a bridle, ornately carved and mounted with silver. Della held it out.

"You want it?"

Karen stared. She focused on the bridle, not wanting to meet her mother's eyes. "It's Galleon's bridle, isn't it."

Della came in and sat down on a corner of the bed. She lay the bridle on the spread between them. "You might as well have it. It's not doing anybody any good on my closet shelf, and if you're going to have a horse of your own . . . You may have to get it cut down to fit a little mare. Galleon was seventeen hands and he had a head like an elephant."

Karen reached out to touch the carved black leather, the silver conches. It was the most beautiful bridle she'd ever seen. On her bay mare's little Arabian head . . .

But it had been Galleon's.

"You better keep it," she said finally. "Thanks anyway."

Della's face became closed and her features tightened. "Okay, if you don't want it. But you remember what I told you when this horse business first came up. It's going to be your responsibility; every penny that that horse costs you is going to have to come out of your money. Saddle, bridle, vet bills, shoeing, it's all going to be up to you. And you're going to have to pay Grampa for hay and grain."

Karen turned away, wishing her mother would leave. Everything always had to turn into a lecture. She wanted to be alone.

Della got up and collected the bridle. She stood for a moment, irresolute, then left. Karen turned out the light, dropped her clothes onto the floor, and crawled into bed. She tried to focus again on the bay mare, and for a while she succeeded, but as sleep approached and relaxed her control, her thoughts strayed once more to Galleon.

With absolute clarity she remembered when her

16

mother first told her about Galleon. Karen was eight. They had just moved from Gramma's house to the trailer, and Karen was watching her mother unpack. The photograph of Galleon surfaced, and Karen snatched it. Even at eight her passion for horses had begun to make itself known, between Karen and her mother.

"Who is that?" Karen demanded.

"That's me, honey."

"No, I didn't mean the lady, I meant the horse."

Della stopped unpacking and settled back with Karen against her leg, to look at the picture. "His name was Galleon. A galleon is a huge, beautiful old Spanish ship, and galleons carried gold to Spain from the New World when Columbus discovered America, and the horse was great big, and beautiful, and gold. So his name was Galleon."

"Was he yours?" Karen stared up at her mother, wide-eyed.

"Yes. He was. For a while."

"What happened to him."

"I sold him. Let's get back to work here, or we'll never get unpacked."

"You *sold* him? Mommy, *why*? How could you ever sell him? Didn't you love him?"

"Of course I did. I didn't want to sell him, honey, but I had to."

But Karen knew, fiercely, that there was no reason good enough to explain selling your own horse, if you were lucky enough to have one. Knowing in a vague way that it would hurt, she asked, "Did you sell my daddy, too?"

Della tried to hug her, but Karen twisted away. "Of course not, sweetheart. People don't sell people."

"But you sold your horse. Didn't you know you were going to have a daughter that would want him, and love him? You should have saved him for me." She began to puddle up and sniffle.

Della pulled her close, and this time Karen allowed her to. "Listen, punkin, I don't know if you're old enough to understand all this, but I had to sell Galleon so I could have you. I found out I was going to have a baby, you, and that costs a lot of money and I didn't have anyone to help me. The horse was the only thing I had, and I wanted to keep him, but I wanted you even more. So I sold him. Now do you understand any better?"

"I guess so," Karen pulled away. She left the room quietly, to absorb this tremendous burden, this overwhelming new guilt.

❊ Three ❊

Karen tried to will herself to sleep, to hurry the morning, but the harder she tried the more tensely awake her mind remained.

She fantasized about the little bay mare.

She thought, warmly, about Harley.

She replayed her first strong memories of him.

She was eleven, and she had a secret obsession. Galleon. From the shaded grays of the newspaper picture the horse had grown, in Karen's mind, into a godlike golden creature. Owning such a horse would elevate anyone far above the level of ordinary people. And her mother, Della Marie Kohler, had owned him.

She had given him up, in order to have her daughter. This part of it was still a bit unclear to Karen. Other people seemed to have children without major sacrifices, but then, she reasoned, other people had

19

husbands, and maybe that made the difference. But although the details of the trade were somewhat hazy in Karen's mind, the central fact stood out painfully clear.

It was her fault that her mother no longer had Galleon.

This fact explained a lot. It explained why her mother didn't love her. It explained why, sometimes in the evenings when the two were forced into each other's company, Della grew restless and unhappy and had to go out for the evening, sending Karen next door or taking her out to Gramma's and Grampa's for the night. It was clear to the miserable child that the sight of her reminded her mother too painfully of the horse she had given up, in order to have this disappointing and unattractive daughter.

By the time Karen was eleven she knew that she would have to try to find Galleon and, somehow, get him back for her mother. It was the only way Della could ever forgive her daughter for the sacrifice of her birth.

Karen began saving her allowances, her birthday money, and even occasionally her Sunday School quarters intended for the offering plate.

Next she approached her mother with painful but necessary questions. "Who did you sell Galleon to, Mom?"

"Harley Williams. Why?"

"Does he still have him?"

"No, honey, Harley doesn't keep horses, he just

buys them and sells them, and that was twelve years ago."

"But Galleon is still alive, isn't he?" A new fear assailed Karen. Maybe it was too late.

"How should I know?"

"How old would he be, by now?"

"You sure ask a lot of strange questions. What's gotten into you today? Oh all right, let me think, he'd be about seventeen, eighteen, around there."

Relief washed over Karen. She wasn't too late. "Horses live that long, don't they?" She spoke with happy confidence.

"Yes, they can live that long. Now would you drop the subject?"

The next part of Karen's plan was much harder. She had to stalk Harley Williams. By coasting casually through the streets of Sand Hills on her bike, watching always for the red stock truck with the "Here Comes Harley" sign, Karen grew familiar with Harley's travel patterns. Evenings through mid-mornings the truck was usually parked in the alley behind the beauty shop, meaning that Harley was either up there, in the apartment over the shop, where she knew he lived with his wife, or else he was in the tavern around the corner. Neither was a place where Karen could, or would, go to talk to him.

Sometimes during the day the truck would head out the main highway, to disappear for hours and often for days. But often it went south on the old blacktop, then returned a few hours later. It was down that road somewhere, Karen deduced, that Harley kept his horses. And that was where she would find him, all alone, and talk to him.

One day she followed the truck on her bike through town and onto the blacktop. She pumped as hard as she could in an effort to keep up, but the truck shrank to a dot and disappeared into the vanishing point on the flat, sweeping landscape.

On she rode, her little chin set grimly. The sun bore down on the barren earth, and rebounded in shimmering heat waves that distorted fence posts and yellow blooming prickly pears. On either side of the road stretched limitless clumps of sparse sand grass, broken here and there by sagebrush or greasewood bushes. Except for an occasional jackrabbit exploding from the grass, Karen was alone.

Alone.

She sweated and pedaled for what seemed an incredibly long time, deciding often to turn back, but continuing anyway. And eventually she was rewarded.

There was a ranch lane, a sign that said, "Harley Williams, Horses Bought and Sold," and beyond was the red truck, parked under a cottonwood tree near a barn and corral.

Karen dropped her bike in the cottonwood's shade, and looked around, panting. With her shirttail she wiped the most annoying sweat from her face and, looking up, met Harley's eyes. He was coming toward her from the barn, not looking particularly surprised but smiling pleasantly enough. It occurred to Karen, in that flash of time, that anyone who owned this many horses was probably used to having kids hanging around. The thought angered her. She did not want to be lumped in with all those others. She was here on important business.

"Well now, where'd you hop in from, jackrabbit?"

As he came close, Karen was overwhelmed by the size, by the grandeur of the man. It was the first time she had seen him up close, although she had always known who he was, had often seen him from a distance, around town. But here he was, close up now, towering over her, his big hat seeming to shade both of them. His deep pale eyes glowed down at her, and his smile beamed sunshine. An ache welled up in Karen, a hunger for something she couldn't even name.

"From town," she managed to say at last. "I followed you."

"You did! Well, bless my buffalo, that's quite a ways to come. What can I do for you?"

Karen gathered her breath. "I'm Karen Kohler. Della Kohler's daughter. You know my mom."

"You're little Karen Kohler? Last time I saw you, you were in diapers. Now here you are, a young lady already." He clucked his tongue and shook his head, and smiled.

"I need your help with something. It's important."

"Well then, young lady, step into my office and make

yourself comfortable." He settled himself on an up-turned bucket, and motioned Karen to a seat on the fender of his truck.

From her elevated viewpoint, Karen looked down at the man and felt a sudden, startling desire to curl herself into his lap. She forgot why she was here.

"Now then," Harley said, "what can I help you with?"

"You don't by any chance still have Galleon, do you?" Her mind came back to the mission at hand.

"Have who? What?"

"Galleon," Karen repeated. "You know. My mother's palomino parade horse. She sold him to you."

The smooth leather face wrinkled in thought. "Oh, yeah, I remember him. But that's been years and years ago. You didn't think I still had him around, did you?"

At the sight of Karen's face, Harley softened his tone. "How come you to be asking about him now?"

"I need to get him back. For my mom. Do you remember who you sold him to?"

"Honey, that's been since before you were born, and I buy and sell probably two, three hundred horses a year. I can't keep track of where they all go to."

"No, I guess not." Karen looked away, fighting back tears of disappointment and humiliation at what seemed to her, now, to be a foolish, childish idea.

"Why don't you tell me why you're looking for that particular horse?" Harley asked. The kindness in his voice eased Karen's pain.

She felt open toward him, trusting, as she had

never felt before toward anyone except her mother, and less and less frequently with her.

"I have to find Galleon," she said, taking a deep breath, "so I can buy him back. For my mother. See, she had to sell him so she could pay for me being born. And now she wishes she hadn't, because I didn't turn out all that great, I guess. Anyway, it was because of me that she had to give up her horse, so it's up to me to get him back for her."

The man's face was such a study in astonishment that Karen broke off and grew silent.

"You listen here," Harley said, "there ain't no mama or no papa in the world that wouldn't give up anything they owned for their children."

"Even a palomino parade horse?" Karen asked in a small voice.

His laugh was as big and beautiful as the man himself. "Even a hundred palomino parade horses. The whole damn Rose Bowl Parade, floats and all."

They laughed together, and the day was glorious.

"And I'll tell you something more," Harley went on. "I remember the day your mama brought me that horse. 'Harley,' she says, 'I'm going to have a little baby and I need some money to make a good home and a good life for that baby. I'm hoping it's going to be a girl, because I want a daughter more than anything in the world. Would you sell my horse for me?'

"And I says, 'That's a fine animal, shame to have to give him up,' and she says, 'Yes, he is, but I already love my baby so much I'd give up anything for it.' "

25

Karen glowed. "Did she really say that?"

He nodded. "And later on, after you were born and all these years while you been growing up, every time I run into Della she starts in bragging about that wonderful little girl of hers. And I'll tell you something else, if my wife and I could have had a daughter like you, I'd have been the happiest man in the world."

Karen was struck silent by the fantasy that filled her mind, Harley Williams as her father.

Abruptly Harley stood. "Come and see my critters."

They walked over to the corral fence, and Karen climbed it for a clear look at the horses beyond. They filled her heart with their shaggy, dusty beauty. There were a dozen or so, in shades of brown, a bony pinto, a small gray donkey, and a shining buckskin who detached himself from the herd and came toward them. He was bigger than the others, and showed signs of some grooming on his dappled gold coat, his black legs and tail, and the line of black down the crest of his neck, where his mane had been clipped off down to the skin.

"This one's my own," Harley said as he ducked through the fence poles to meet the horse. "This one ain't for sale. Raised him from a colt, and nobody rides him but me, ever."

He gripped the horse's shorn neck and leaped onto him. With a hearty slap to the animal's neck, he turned him away from the fence and sent him cantering around the corral. Karen marveled. With a loud "whoa" Harley brought the horse to a sliding stop in front of Karen. He jumped to the ground and said, "I tell you what. I've never let anyone else ride Sunny before, but I think you're a pretty special girl. You hop on him and take him for a little ride."

"Me?"

"Who else would I be talking to out here, the rabbits?"

"Without a saddle or bridle, or anything to hang onto?"

"He'll behave for you if I tell him to."

Wide-eyed, Karen jumped down inside the fence, and approached the horse. He towered over her head. With an easy motion Harley ankled her up onto the high, smooth, golden back.

"Just slap his neck like you were neck-reining. He'll go along for you."

This was Karen's fourth time on a horse. The other rides had been on a neighbor's pony, with reins for control and a saddle horn for security. And the ground much nearer. But Harley was standing there, watching. She couldn't fail in his eyes.

"Let's go, Sunny." She slapped the neck, timidly, and gave an infinitesimal squeeze with her legs. There was a tuft of mane left untrimmed, over the horse's withers. She grabbed it and hung on. They went at a walk three times around the corral, the horse stopping on his own each time they came back to Harley. By the third round Karen was relaxed and loving the ride. She wanted it to go on, but Harley was reaching up for her, so she slid obediently into his grasp.

"Thank you for letting me ride him," she breathed.

"You got the makings of a good little rider. You ought to have a horse of your own."

"I know. I want one. Awful bad. But I was saving my money for Galleon—"

"If I was you," Harley said frankly, "I'd forget all about that idea, and use that money to get yourself a nice little horse."

"I've only got thirty dollars," Karen said in a small voice.

He laughed. "Well, that's not much of a start, but it's a start. You keep saving up, and when the time comes, you let ole Harley know, and I'll find the horse for you."

That was four years ago, and the scene still played vividly in Karen's mind. "When the time comes," he had said. It had taken four years to build that thirty dollars into two hundred, to convince her mother that a horse was a necessity to Karen. To talk Gramma and Grampa into promising to let her keep her horse out there, when the time came.

And now, the time had come.

The little bay mare waited, handpicked by Harley, who loved her.

✕ Four ✕

"Tell me everything about her," Karen said as she settled herself on the truck seat and slammed the door. "Is she a blood bay?"

"What do you mean by that, blood bay?" Harley asked.

She looked at him to see if he was kidding. "You know, bright red, like in that book, *The Blood Bay Colt.*"

"Well, no, she's—a mahogany bay. That's the darker brown kind, almost black."

Karen sadly parted with her vision of bright red hide against black points. But mahogany sounded pretty, too.

They passed the town limits, and the truck gathered speed. Harley glanced sideways at Karen, then said, "Now this little mare's not in her best condition right now. She's a little thin, and she's going a little sore-

29

footed because her hooves have been let to grow out away too long. Nothing a little good care won't fix up, but I thought I'd better tell you about it. Y'see, it's kind of a sad story. The people I bought her from—"

"I thought you bought her at an auction."

"No, honey, I wouldn't let you have an auction horse. These were some people I knew, back when I used to live around Saint Jo. I knew what their situation was, so I gave them a call when I was in town, this trip, and sure enough, the mare was for sale. I've had her in mind for you for quite some time now, but I didn't want to say anything, because of their situation."

"What situation?" Karen didn't realize she was bouncing on the truck seat.

"The little mare belonged to their daughter, y'see. She was a sweet little thing, about your age, and crazy for horses, just like you. Only thing was, she had this disease. I can't just recall the name of it, but she was born with it, and they knew she couldn't live too long. She could get around, but she was weak, and they had to be careful of her.

"Cathy, that was her name, kept begging for a horse, and her folks couldn't hardly say no to anything she wanted that bad, so they said okay, even though they didn't have much money. They took her to look at a few horses, and as soon as Cathy saw Lady Bay, that's your mare's name—"

A thrill shot through Karen.

"—it was love at first sight. But the mare hadn't been broke to ride, so Cathy's folks said no, she'd have to find her a different one. But that little Cathy, she walked over to the mare, kinda looked at her for a minute, and then climbed up on her back, and the mare just stood there, as mild as morning milk. Cathy'd never been on a horse, and the mare had never been rode, but the two of them just seemed to have some special kind of communication."

"Like ESP?" Karen's voice went high with excitement.

"Maybe. Anyway, they bought the mare for Cathy. She rode her for just that one summer, and then she was too sick to ride, but they kept the horse right there in their backyard, where she and Cathy could see each other through the bedroom window."

"Cathy died?"

Harley nodded. "A few months ago. Her folks, they were pretty broke up about it, as you can imagine. They put off selling the horse, 'cause Cathy'd loved it so much. And they were afraid Lady Bay might go to somebody that would mistreat her. But on the other hand, neither of them knew diddly about taking care of a horse. They didn't keep her feet trimmed like they should have, and they didn't buy her any extra feed when the yard ran low on grass."

"So they finally decided to sell her to you."

"But only because of one thing. Well, two things. They needed the money pretty bad, all those years of hospital bills, and then the funeral. But when I told them about you, that clinched the deal. I told them you'd love that little mare just like Cathy did."

The truck bumped off of the blacktop and up to the ranch road, and coasted to a stop under the cotton-wood. Karen was already out. She felt almost dizzy as she approached the corral, the combined effect of Harley's story and the immenseness of the moment. Meeting her horse. For there was no question that Lady Bay was to be hers.

She ducked through the fence rails and stood, for-getting even Harley. Of the dozen or so horses in the corral, three were dark brown, but Karen recognized Lady Bay instantly.

The mare was standing somewhat apart from the others, her head low, her back slightly arched, her hind legs angled forward as though to ease the weight from her front feet. The front hooves were shockingly long, their forward growth bearing a grotesque sim-ilarity to human feet.

Karen felt pain in her chest, as though her heart were literally going out, out of herself, to the mare. She went to the mare and put her arms around the low-hung neck.

"You're mine now, Lady Bay. I could just kill them for letting you get like this, but it's all over now. I'll get you all fixed up, and I'll love you just as much as Cathy did, and you'll love me."

She stroked the mane, the bony shoulder, the rib-ridged side.

32

The mare leaned the weight of her head on Karen's arm and sighed.

Harley said, "She's an awful sweet little mare. You'll need to get those feet trimmed, so she can walk right, before you ride her, is the only thing. I'd have had the farrier out to do it today, but he couldn't come till tomorrow and I knew you'd be itching to see her."

Karen turned to him, but didn't let go of the horse's neck. "How much is she?"

"Well, now, I give Cathy's folks four hundred for her, so that's what I'll have to price her at, but I won't charge you any extra, like I would for anybody else, for hauling her from Missouri or for my profit. You can have her for the four hundred, and you can just give me what you've got now, and pay the rest as you get it. How's that sound?"

Four hundred sounded huge, to someone who had spent four years amassing two hundred. *But,* Karen thought quickly, *now that I've got regular baby-sitting jobs it'll come in faster, and by next summer I can probably get a job in a restaurant or somewhere. I can do it. I'd do anything for her.*

"If you can take two hundred down, then—"

He grinned and shook her hand. "Then you got yourself a horse, young lady. Shall we load her up?"

Harley fetched a cheap rope halter from the truck. "Here, you can keep that if you want."

The simple act of slipping the halter on her mare's head brought a trembling happiness to Karen. It was a gesture of possession. Later, when she could afford

33

them, there would be a bridle, a saddle, the inexplicable magic of buckling a throatlatch, pulling up a cinch. Whenever she wanted to. On her own horse.

It was such a magnificent leap from being one of the envious ones who stood watching while the lucky neighbor saddled his pony, put his toe in the stirrup with the arrogance of ownership, and rode away.

Such a leap should be taken gradually, Karen thought. It would be too much happiness to bear if it came all at once. Now there was the horse, the halter. The rest would follow later.

While Harley backed the truck into the loading chute Karen led her mare, by slow, painful steps, across the corral. Lady Bay followed, resigned to whatever might be coming.

They drove more slowly back toward town, in consideration of their sore-footed passenger. Downtown, they stopped in front of the bank while Karen ran inside and withdrew her money. "I'm buying a horse," she said to the teller, who tried to show some interest.

Then they drove out of town again, west a mile then south a short distance.

"It's that next place," Karen said, pointing.

Her grandparents' farm was not large by Colorado standards, but it appeared tidy and well cared for. There was a stucco house, small and square and painted a soft green, with low tamarisk trees offering shade and pink blossoms. Flower borders rimmed the lawn, while fences ran in taut wire-lines around the pasture. The outbuildings were painted the same green as the house, and stood in flawless repair.

No one came out to greet them as the truck drew to a stop in the turnaround behind the house. "Gramma's at work," Karen explained. "Grampa's probably out with his cattle somewhere. His dog's not here." She felt oddly relieved, and she fancied that Harley did, too. For an instant she wondered if he could be shy of meeting new people, like she was. It was an endearing thought.

When the mare was unloaded and turned loose to stumble across the mud clods in the barnyard, Harley said, "I've got to get back to town. You want to ride in with me, or stay here?"

"Oh, I'll stay here. I can walk back. Thanks. Thanks for everything, Harley, for finding Lady Bay for me—" Her voice trembled.

"Ah," he waved her aside, "don't thank me. It was my pleasure." He remounted the truck and drove away, the ten twenty-dollar bills making a bulge in his shirt pocket.

With a tender kind of joy Karen brought out from the barn an armload of hay, then a bucket of oats. The mare ate as though she were starving. Karen watched for a while, smiling gently, then she turned and ran to the house, suddenly eager to get those hooves trimmed, to remove the pain from Lady Bay's stance.

To ride.

The phone was on the kitchen counter. She looked up farriers in the yellow pages, found only one, dialed the number. The man's wife answered, said he was out making calls but that she could probably catch him on the truck's radio and he might have time to come that afternoon.

It was late afternoon before anyone drove in. Karen turned from her perch on the barn lot fence, eager for the hoof-trimming to be done. There was still time for a little ride before supper. But it was her grandfather's pickup, not the farrier's truck. Willard Kohler saw Karen, and came toward her, his Australian cattle dog close behind him.

"Come and see my horse, Grampa. I just got her."

He was a large man, bald and bullet-headed and thick through the neck. He wore his town clothes, boots and clean jeans and a blue shirt open at the neck. His face was unsmiling, but no more so than usual. Still, Karen quaked a little before him, realizing suddenly how her horse would look to this no-nonsense stockman.

He walked into the barn lot, stopped, looked hard at the mare. His expression didn't change but his voice was hard.

"How much did you get took for?"

"She just needs to have her feet trimmed, and she's a little thin right now. But there's a reason."

"There always is, Karen." He managed to make her name sound like an insult.

"No, really, Grampa. These people that owned her,

36

their daughter died, and Lady Bay was the daughter's horse, the parents didn't know anything about taking—"

"How much?"

"Grampa, please—"

"How much, Karen? And who bummed her off onto you?"

"Harley Williams. I gave him two hundred." She didn't dare say the two hundred was only half-payment. Everything was going sour. She willed Grampa to leave her alone with Lady Bay.

"You paid him two hundred dollars for this animal? Then he's a crook and you're a fool, girl. An old foundered thing like this he probably picked up at some sale for fifty, sixty bucks. He sure saw you coming."

"What do you mean? And what do you mean, 'foundered'?"

Just then the farrier arrived. He was a young man, smiling until he saw the mare. "Wow, she's awful bad foundered, isn't she? Well, we'll see what we can do."

Grampa left them alone. Karen held the mare's head while the farrier picked up one front foot and tapped it gently with a small hammer. The mare pulled back and sucked in her breath.

"How'd she do it?" the man asked as he set to work with nippers, biting away inches of excess hoof.

"I just bought her, this morning. I don't even know what foundered means," Karen said miserably. "Is she going to get better?"

He turned to look up at her, over his shoulder. His expression showed pity. "Let me guess. Harley Williams sold her to you, right?"

"How did you know?"

He let the question go, and said instead, "A horse can founder itself different ways, eating too much grain, eating or drinking when they're hot, that sort of thing. Ponies'll founder quite often in the spring, from too much richness in the grass that time of the year. Or a mare can founder if she has a foal and doesn't clean afterward, that is, if some of the afterbirth stays inside the mare and causes an infection."

"But," Karen motioned to the crippled feet.

"What happens is that there's a swelling in the tissue that lies between the outer shell of the hoof and the inner bones of a horse's feet, and since neither the hoof nor the bones have any room to give, the swelling is terribly painful for the horse. In bad cases like this, the hoof will pull away from the foot completely, and the hoof grows way faster than ordinary. See how she's standing, kind of humped over, with her hind legs under her body? She's trying to get as much weight as possible off these front feet, because that's where the trouble is. And see, here, these bony rings of growth on the outside wall of her hooves, that means she's been foundered before, several times. Some horses are just chronic founderers."

"Will she be okay?" Karen ceased breathing.

He stood and shifted his weight to the other front foot. The trimmed one looked almost normal now.

"She'll get better for now, but you'll always have to watch her extra careful, and even then it'll probably come back from time to time. I'll come out every two, three weeks, and keep trimming back on these hooves. Your vet will probably have to soak her feet in cold water. That helps take away the swelling and pain. She's not ever going to run in the Kentucky Derby, but we'll get her so you can ride her anyway."

When he was gone, Karen led the mare to the pasture and released her. Then she sat on the grass and watched while Lady Bay, walking somewhat more comfortably, put her head down to graze.

Karen's mind was crowded with thought she wasn't ready to face. Not yet. She couldn't think about Harley, couldn't wonder how a professional horse trader had failed to recognize a foundered horse when her grandfather had spotted it, right off, and he wasn't a horse lover.

≫ Five ≫

On Main Street, between the movie theater and the jewelry store, was a very small office whose window was gold-lettered, "Allied Mutual Insurance." The blue-and-green striped carpet, the white walls, the New York skyline picture opposite the sunburst clock, all seemed a quixotic attempt at urbanity in Sand Hills, Colorado.

But Della liked it. Her desk was angled toward the window so she could smile at passersby while she typed or talked on the phone. There was a certain prestige attached to working here. It was a definite step up, socially, from clerking at Sears. Sears was fine for her mother, who had been there in Linens and Draperies for as long as Della could remember, and was content there because it got her into town and among people three and a half days a week. But then, her mother had never had to live down unpleasant gossip, and prove herself.

As she was slipping the gray plastic cover over her typewriter, Della's phone rang.

"Good afternoon, Allied Mutual."

"Oh, Della. I'm glad I caught you before you left."

"Hi, Mother."

"Listen, Della, Karen's out here with her new horse, and she's going to need a ride home, so why don't you come out for supper? That'll give Karen a little more time to pet the horse, and I know you're anxious to see it. My, is she excited. So why don't you come on out?"

Della stalled and studied the sunburst clock. She knew she would have to go. There was no way out of it. "Okay, look, Mom, I've got to work a little late tonight. It'll be probably an hour or so before I can get finished up here."

"That's all right, dear. I just got home myself, and it'll take that long for the potatoes to bake. You just come on when you can."

Della hung up the phone and fished her purse from the typewriter well. "Be okay if I leave a few minutes early?" she called, and the voice from the back office answered, "No problem. See you in the morning."

She left her car where it was and walked to the end of the block and around the corner to the bar. A little Dutch courage, she told herself as she settled in at her favorite table, halfway back in the long narrow room.

She smiled and lifted her fingers to Max, and he brought her a tall frosty beer, spilling foam.

But why should I need Dutch courage, just to go out to my folks' for supper, for heaven's sake? she asked herself. *That's stupid. It's because of Karen, isn't it, and the horse. Because all these years she's had the idea I was some kind of hot-shot horse expert and I don't want her to find out different. And, let's face it, it hurts a little bit when your kid goes out and does something as big as buying a horse, and doesn't even bother to tell you about it. They stopped at the bank, right practically across the street from my office. It wouldn't have taken her two minutes to run over and tell me about the horse. If we were as close as we should be, that's what she would have done.*

Until recently Della had ricocheted through her life, bouncing off of events and people. It was only in the last year or so that she had begun looking into her own mind, attempting to analyze her moods and her needs. Maybe it was because there was more time, now, to think and reflect. Her early years had been too full of immediate crises to allow for anything more than just reacting.

Caught undressed with an eighteen-year-old boy when she was thirteen, Della had reacted to her father's rage by learning to get out of the house through her bedroom window.

Caught again a few years later, with a ranch hand and part-time rodeo rider, she reacted by taking Gal-

42

leon out for a Saturday morning ride, meeting the ranch hand out on the highway, loading Galleon into his horse trailer, and setting off for the rodeo circuit. She had laughed at her father, cried a little for her mother, and set her sights on the fantastically fun life ahead of her.

A few months later she was caught again, this time by pregnancy. The fun was over. Pregnant girls can't earn their share of expenses barrel-racing, nor win prestige as rodeo queen for their men. Crisis and expediency forced Della to do something she didn't, deep down, want to do.

But now, finally, the events of Della's life had slowed to a controllable speed. She'd had the same job for several years now, and it fitted her. It supplied her with enough money to live on and a slot, on a comfortable level, in Sand Hills society. There were boyfriends, not always when she needed one, but pretty consistently, and they were decent guys.

And there was Karen.

Della frowned and shredded her damp napkin, thinking about last night.

Why on earth wouldn't she take Galleon's bridle? Here she is, buying her first horse, all excited about it, and I offer her a silver mounted bridle, for nothing, and she won't take it. That kid has always acted a little funny about Galleon. Sometimes I almost get the feeling she knows about—why I sold him. But that's impossible. Nobody but Harley knows about that,

43

nobody around Sand Hills anyway, and Karen was acting funny about the subject of Galleon long before she ever crossed paths with Harley Williams. So I'm sure she doesn't know.

Well, think of the devil, Della said to herself. Harley had arrived, bringing fresh air and heartiness into the dim, quiet place. He started toward the bar, saw Della, hesitated. In the shadowy light it was hard for Della to be sure, but Harley's expression seemed guarded.

Della smiled. "I hear you did a little business with my daughter today," she said, expecting him to join her at her table.

"Yep," he said. "Give me a six-pack of Coors to go, will you, Max?"

"Why don't you stay and have a beer with me?" Della said. "I'm just on my way out to the folks' for supper. And, of course, to see Karen's horse. I guess she was pretty excited this morning, wasn't she?"

Harley stroked back the silver waves over his ears, and shook his head at Max, who was poised to draw a glass of draft. "I can't stay. Got to get on home to the little woman, you know. Yeah, Karen liked the little mare, right off. Horse'd had some bad care, lately, Karen'll tell you all about it. But she's a nice gentle little mare, that's the main thing. I knew you'd want me to pick something safe for Karen, and that's what I did. Got to keep my girl happy, don't I?" he

44

rumpled Della's hair. It would have been as impossible for Harley not to flirt as it would have for Della.

"I'm not your girl, never was, and you know it. All the crowds of women around you, I never figured I could hack my way through all that competition."

"Aw," he grinned, "it was the other way around, honey. All them younger guys, an old duffer like me never had a chance."

The exchange cheered them both. Harley left and Della sank back into her own thoughts. She remembered Harley Williams as she first knew him, seventeen, eighteen years ago. Della Kohler was the hotshot kid with the big palomino and the cute little figure and the mass of long curls. Harley was the local horse trader, the big, good-looking guy with salt-and-pepper hair and the wife whom no one ever saw, at least no one among the Sand Hills horsey set, the quarter horse people, the Saddle Club trail riders, the ranch hands who liked to play rodeo on weekends. Harley was the big voice, the big stories with a hollow ring to them.

Sure he was magnetic, and sure Della flirted with him, every chance she got. But somehow it never went beyond that. Della's instincts warned her away from Harley. There was something insubstantial about the man. And, of course, with her looks and reputation, Della Kohler had never needed to resort to middle-aged men.

45

The bar began to fill up. A few truckers, a couple of workers from the packing plant, people putting off going home for their own varied reasons. Della looked at the clock, sighed, and got up. At the cash register she took the precaution of buying a roll of lifesavers to cover her beer breath. Then she got into her car and headed it grimly toward the family dinner.

✖ Six ✖

Willard and Etta Kohler stood at the living-room window and watched their daughter and grand-daughter drive away. Then, together, they went into the kitchen and set to work. They worked automatically, smoothly. He scraped plates into the dog's dish and put away leftovers, while she ran the dishwasher and began on the silverware and glasses.

They were both exhausted by the tensions of the dinner, Willard's anger toward Della for allowing her daughter to be cheated, Della's defensive snappiness, Etta's unhappy attempts at smoothing things over, and under it all, Karen's frenetic but defensive excitement about the horse.

"Maybe we shouldn't interfere," Etta said.

Willard grew noisier in his dish scraping. "Somebody's got to look out for that child's interest. If her mother doesn't care enough about her to—"

"Now, Will, you know perfectly well Della adores Karen. She said she felt it was important to let Karen have this experience on her own, buying the horse. There is something to be said for letting young people learn from their mistakes, you know."

He looked at her with an old bitterness, and she grew quiet.

Willard said, "I never did trust that Harley Williams, anyway. Any man that'd live off what his wife earned, and spend his life playing cowboy—because that's exactly what he does, you know. He just plays at things. No more sense of responsibility than a billy goat. If Della knew Karen was buying her horse from that man, she should have warned the child. She should have looked at the horse herself before any money changed hands."

Etta snorted, and reached for the stack of pans to be washed. "I don't know as that would have done any good. Della's no authority on horses. And any man that'd smile at her, she'd buy anything he was selling. Her watching out for Karen in a horse deal would be like sending the goose to guard the hen-house. How bad is the horse, really?"

Willard finished clearing the table, and began drying the silverware. He shuffled each piece into its stall in the drawer, punctuating his words with metallic clashes.

"The mare is old, she's thin, and she's foundered. A good worming and plenty of food will probably put some weight on her, and the age isn't necessarily a

48

drawback, not in a beginner's horse. The feet, I don't know. I expect they can be got back into good enough shape so Karen can ride, but with chronic founder, the mare is going to be lame on and off, the rest of her life."

"How do you know it's chronic?"

His voice grew louder in anger, not at his wife but at the situation. "Because it shows, on her hooves. You can see rings on them, like extra growth of the hoof, from other times she's foundered. We had a horse like that when I was a kid, and we finally had to have him butchered. Couldn't work him, couldn't ride him most of the time, couldn't sell him. At least, not honestly," he ended bitterly.

"Well, at least Karen seems happy, and I guess that's the main thing. She needed an animal to love, and she's got it now."

They worked silently for a minute, then Etta said, "And thank goodness Karen hasn't started getting interested in boys yet. I hope to heaven this horse will keep her mind off of all that, for a few years anyway."

"It surely didn't do any good with Della." Pain sharpened his words. "The fanciest horse in the country, we bought for her. And look how that ended up."

"Well, that's true. Maybe that was our mistake. Maybe if we hadn't got her such a flashy horse she wouldn't have drawn so much attention from the men."

But neither of them believed that.

Willard shook his head. "The devil got an early

49

hold on that girl. Sunday School and church every week of her life while she was under our roof, and it didn't do a bit of good. We raised her the best we could, Mother, and she went bad anyway. I think it's time we quit blaming ourselves for how she turned out."

Etta released the dish water and rinsed the suds from her hands and arms. "Turned out. I don't think she's turned out all that bad. She was wild when she was young, and she had a baby when maybe she shouldn't have, but she's a good girl now. She works hard, supports herself and Karen, and I don't ever hear any talk about her, in town."

"Well, that's a blessing anyway," he said, somewhat mollified. He hung up his dish towel and took the dog's dish out to the back steps. The dog appeared instantly.

The sky was fully black now, except for a lighter shading beyond the mountains in the distance, but a brilliant abundance of stars illuminated Willard's world. The familiar shapes of barn and fences, of yearling calves gathered near the feeder and a glow-eyed cat stalking in the long grass, all soothed the man and reassured him. He fished his pipe from his shirt pocket, and began the ritual of packing and lighting it.

For many years Willard had wanted a son, and then had mourned when it became obvious that he would not father one, and that Della was not going to provide him with a son-in-law, or a grandson. He had, in his early years, imagined himself growing old in gradual stages while teaching a son to love the ranch, and to care for it as he had, teaching him about rotating pastureland and hay fields, how to time the hay cuttings and how to recognize screwworm before it damaged the herd. He imagined himself retiring in his late sixties, maybe traveling a little, taking the wife on one of those group tours to the Holy Land if they could afford it.

But now that his late sixties were here, he found himself almost glad that there was no son, no grandson. Willard Kohler still ran this place. He still made every decision, from buying a bull to ordering fencing staples. He felt as young as he ever had, and he recognized the fact that he would have hated handing the place over to a son, or anyone else.

It was still his home, his ranch. His family. His family to protect and care for, even though Della refused his care, as she always had. But there was Karen.

Cradling his pipe in his palm, Willard walked across the yard to the pasture gate. The mare was grazing near the fence.

He approached, and she watched his approach calmly, with head raised, but jaws still chewing.

For some time Willard stood sucking on his pipe and looking thoughtfully at the mare. He was a cattleman; his knowledge of horses was peripheral, facts picked up here and there around the edges of the cattle business. Horses had been, on occasion, helpful tools in working with the cattle. They had never been pets.

He shook his head and turned to go. The mare followed him back to the pasture gate, seeking the reassurance of his company in this strange place. At the gate Willard paused and gave her neck a pat, then went to the barn and brought her a measure of oats.

"I sure hope you don't let that little girl down," he muttered.

A sudden resolve hardened Willard's face. He went into the house and picked up the phone book.

"Who are you calling at this hour?" Etta asked. She paused in her dishing up of Willard's bedtime ice cream.

"That man cheated our granddaughter, and I'm not going to sit still for it." He found the number, held it with one calloused finger, and dialed.

"Hello, let me talk to Harley Williams."

Etta caught her breath. She hated unpleasantness among the people around her, and this felt like trouble.

"Well, where is he, do you know? I want to talk to him—now. . . . All right, I'll try there."

Willard hung up and consulted the phone book again. "What's the name of that bar, anyhow?"

For a weeknight, Max's Bar was well filled. Max and his two waitresses were in constant motion, and the music seemed to ricochet from the wall. Smoke hung in the air.

Harley stood at the bar, leaning sideways against its padded rim so that he could give full attention to the girl on the stool. She was probably too young to be served legally, but neither Max nor the Sand Hills authorities were overly concerned about such things. Her face was thin-featured but brightly made-up, and she had a lively look that Harley recognized and played to. Her boyfriend, on the stool beyond her, watched Harley with an equal blend of interest and apprehension.

"Listen," Harley said, "I know how it is, a girl working, living in an apartment, it's not too practical to keep a horse, but if you like to ride you just come out to my place any time at all. I've always got a barn full of horses out there, you can take your pick and ride as much as you want. I'd even let you ride my buckskin. I don't usually let people ride him, but I'd make an exception for you. Pretty little thing like you, I'm sure Sunny'd consider it an honor to carry you. You come too," he said, extending the invitation to the boyfriend with a false sincerity that fooled no one.

The boyfriend's face darkened. "Lisa don't have time to go riding around on horses, so you can keep your invitations to yourself."

Harley gave them both a sparkling smile. "Now, now, just a friendly suggestion. No harm meant there, buddy. Max, let's have another round, here.

Say, boys," Harley raised his voice to carry over the crowd noise to the three-man western band at the end of the room, "how about a little Hank Williams music."

The band members grinned knowingly at one another and struck up, "Your Cheatin' Heart." It was a standing joke among them that when Harley called for Hank Williams music he was moving in for the kill.

Harley lowered his voice to an intimate softness. "I expect you're too young to remember Hank Williams. He was the greatest country-western singer that ever was. He was my uncle, you know."

Lisa's eyes widened. She looked up at him with new respect. "Hank Williams was your uncle? Really? No kidding?"

Harley was just bending himself around her in a protective curve, when Max tapped him on the arm.

"Telephone, Harley."

"Now don't you move, darlin'. I'll be right back, hear?"

Harley took the phone around the corner in the slightly quieter hallway by the rest rooms. "Hello?"

"Harley Williams? Listen here, this is Willard Kohler. You sold my granddaughter a worthless horse this morning, and I want to know what you're going to do about it."

Harley's soft, romantic mood was pierced by the

anger coming at him through the phone. "Now you looka here, that deal was between Karen and me, and you've got no call to—"

"You've got no call to cheat a little girl. She told me she paid you two hundred dollars for that animal, and I know damn well you didn't pay more than fifty or sixty for it. That horse is a chronic founder, you know it and I know it, and now Karen knows it. Do you know how long that little girl saved her pennies to buy a horse? Do you have any idea what that animal means to Karen? Or do you care? Are you just out to make a buck any way you can, and never mind who gets hurt? I pray to God for your soul, that's all I've got to say."

Harley thought quickly. "Foundered, you say? That's a surprise to me, Mr. Kohler. I admit I didn't get a very good look at the little mare's feet, but she was sold to me by some very old and dear friends, so I reckon I didn't look as close as I might have otherwise. I tell you what, I'll refund half of the mare's price. Will that keep everyone happy? I'll take the loss myself. I can absorb it better than that little girl can. I'm surely sorry this happened, Mr. Kohler. You tell Karen if she doesn't want to keep the mare, I'll take her back. That be fair enough?"

There was a silence on the line. Then, reluctantly, Willard said, "I expect," and hung up.

Harley returned to the girl at the bar. Her boyfriend was nowhere in sight.

55

"Who was that, your wife looking for you?" she asked, teasing.

"Just a business call." Harley raised his new drink. "No, my wife doesn't keep track of my comings and goings, and I don't keep track of hers. Makes a nice working arrangement."

The girl lifted her eyebrows. "I just bet."

They laughed together.

❧ Seven ❧

Karen was just leaving home the next morning, on her way to Lady Bay, when the phone rang.

"Karen? Listen, honey, this is Harley. I got to thinking about that mare of yours and I decided maybe I shouldn't have charged you full price for her. Tell you the truth, I didn't take as close a look at her when I bought her as I should have, and her not being in the best of condition right now, well, how would it be if we forget about the two hundred you owe on her, and just call it even?"

The magnanimity of his offer knocked the breath out of Karen. The burden of the future payments seemed to lift and float away.

"But, Harley, you paid four hundred for her. That would mean you'd lose two hundred dollars, just for being nice to me. I don't want you to lose money for my sake."

He laughed, and Karen loved him.

"Now, honey, you don't need to worry about that. I'll just chalk it up to experience. You're my best girl, and I promised to find you a good horse, and I don't want anybody to be able to say old Harley didn't do right by you. Hear?"

She thanked him and hung up, and ran, singing, out of the trailer. Her bike seemed to fly, this morning, along the back streets at the edge of town, through the Mexican section, and out to the highway. Just before Harley's call Karen had phoned the veterinarian. He was to stop by the farm later that morning. Then Lady Bay would start getting better, and Harley hadn't cheated her after all, and it was a glorious day.

Until the fear was lifted, Karen hadn't fully realized the depth of her reaction to her grandfather's words. She had never tried to analyze her feelings for the big, smiling, silver-haired horse trader, but since the afternoon when he assured her that her mother loved her, Harley Williams had assumed a special importance in Karen's life.

At first their contacts were limited to Karen's visits to his ranch. She forced herself to space those visits far enough apart so that she wouldn't become an unwelcome nuisance. She studied his welcomes, and if they seemed genuine, she relaxed and stayed for the afternoon. If someone else were there, buying a horse or talking business, she left and pedaled the three hot miles back to town.

As they got to know each other, Harley began to

let Karen ride a few of the horses for him, particularly the ponies who were too small to carry Harley. Karen rode newly acquired animals and told Harley what they were like, so that he could sell them accordingly: an absolutely safe kids' pony, quick but ornery, needs a tougher rider, likes to buck, or whatever.

There had been times when Karen was thrown, or run away with. Often she was afraid, sickly afraid to get on a horse who had hurt her the day before. But Harley was watching. Harley needed her help with the ponies. And Harley thought that she was as brave a rider as he was himself, and no other fear was stronger than her fear of losing Harley's respect.

And there had been precious moments of closeness during those summer afternoons. Once Karen had asked him why he lived in town, instead of there where his horses were. He explained, in his gentle, intimate voice, that his wife had been sick most of their married life and needed to be close to medical attention. Also, he went on, his wife was not a country person. She would be as unhappy living out here as Harley was living in town, but he was the man, and it was up to him to make the sacrifices.

He went on to tell Karen about his dream, a log ranch house right over there in that cottonwood grove, a big sprawling place with deep porches all around, and stone fireplaces and bear rugs.

Karen felt awed and honored to be the one to whom he told his dreams. She ached for him, because he couldn't live the way he was meant to live, and she developed a resentment that bordered on hatred for Harley's wife, who was spoiling his whole life by refusing to live in the country.

As Karen grew older, and their friendship matured, Harley sometimes took her and a spare horse for her to ride, when the Sand Hills Saddle Club met for trail rides through the ochre and dusty green foothill country. These were times of intense pleasure for Karen, although Harley spent much of his time talking and joking with older people. Women. But as he explained to her once, this was a necessary part of being a professional horse trader. Keeping up friendly contacts, he called it, and Karen understood.

With increasing frequency Harley began taking Karen, and sometimes Della, to the horse sales in the Sand Hills Auction Barn the first Friday of each month. Often Harley allowed her to ride one of his horses into the sale ring, to demonstrate that the horse was kid-broke and "safe for Mom and the younguns," as the auctioneer was fond of saying. Sometimes Karen had her doubts about the safety of a particular horse, but Harley's confidence in her riding ability was a treasure to her, and she wouldn't have risked losing it by declining to ride into the ring.

And tonight was a sale night, Karen thought as she turned her bike from the highway onto Grampa's road. Now that she wouldn't have to make payments on Lady Bay, and if the veterinarian would let her charge till the end of the month, she could probably afford a used bridle if there was one auctioned off tonight for eight dollars or less.

She thought for an instant about Galleon's silver mounted bridle, but she shook her head. The bridle was all her mother had left of the horse she must have loved as Karen now loved Lady Bay. Having been the cause of Della's losing Galleon, and the silver saddle, the very least she could do was not to take the bridle, too.

Karen was relieved to see that her grandfather was nowhere in sight as she rode into the yard. She wanted to tell him that Harley had cut the mare's price in half, but if Grampa pressed for details, he might find out that she'd lied yesterday, in letting him believe that two hundred, not four hundred, was the total price. Better to avoid the whole subject as long as possible.

From the barn Karen got a measure of oats, an old brush, and a lead rope. Lady Bay was waiting near the pasture gate.

"You're happy to see me, aren't you? Did you know you're my horse now? I'm going to take care of you for the rest of your life. Here you go. That's right, eat it all up so you can get nice and fat."

She tied the mare to the gatepost and began brushing in long, slow, dreamy strokes. A huge cottonwood shaded them from the gathering heat of the day. For Karen, this moment was worth everything it had cost, and might cost in the future.

She was brushing her own horse.

With the tip of the brush Karen lovingly traced the mare's white star and stripe down the long bones of the face, gently around eyes and ears, then down the warm neck, lifting the mane to let the breeze in. It occurred to Karen that this was probably the first grooming Lady Bay had had since Cathy died. Tenderness overwhelmed her.

The veterinarian's truck drove in. As he strode toward her, Karen tensed. *What if there was something really wrong with Lady Bay?* she thought in sudden panic.

"This the one?" the man said.

Karen nodded. "My Grampa and the farrier said she'd had founder, and they thought she probably needed worming, too. What do you think?"

He came through the gate and picked up one of Lady Bay's front hooves. When he struck the hoof with his pocket knife, the mare drew back sharply. He lowered her foot, patted her shoulder, glanced at the dull, rough coat and protruding hipbones. Then he went to his truck and came back with a length of rubber hose, and medication.

"What are you going to do with that?" Karen asked, alarmed.

"You hold her head, there. I'm going to run this tube up her nose and all the way down to her stomach, like this," he matched actions to words, "so I can get the worming medicine directly down there where it's needed. After this you can worm her yourself with a paste wormer, just squirt it on her tongue. But for now, she looks to be so loaded with worms that the tube method is best. This animal has been shamefully neglected, little lady."

"I just got her yesterday," Karen said swiftly.

"Then I'm sure she's going to get better care from now on. She's been foundered, and the feet are still pretty sore. That will go away in time. You can speed it along by soaking her feet in cool water, to reduce the inflamation of the laminae, there."

"I will."

"And you'll have to be extra careful with her, so she doesn't founder again. Don't ever let her drink, or eat much, when she's hot. You feel under here," he put his hand in the vee between the mare's front legs, "and if her skin feels warm, don't let her drink. Don't give her more than two, three, quarts of grain a day, don't let her get at any dusty or moldy hay, don't let her eat straw, don't turn her out in rich pasture early in the spring except for just short periods at a time. Keep her hooves trimmed back as far as you can. You got all that?"

Karen nodded.

"Good. Whoever let her get in this shape ought to be horsewhipped."

"It wasn't their fault, really. She belonged to this girl in Missouri who was real sick, and she died a few months ago. She loved Lady Bay more than anything in the world. In fact, Lady Bay had never been ridden, and Cathy, that was the girl's name, just took one look at her and fell in love with her, and got on and started riding her. It was just like some sort of magic between them. But then Cathy got worse, and she was in the hospital a long time, and finally died. And her parents didn't know anything about taking care of a horse, but yet they hated to sell Lady Bay because Cathy had loved her so much."

The man's face softened. "Oh, well, then I guess there were some mitigating circumstances. There's still no excuse for letting a horse get in this kind of shape, but in a case like that..."

He gathered his things and started toward the truck.

"How soon can I ride her?"

"Soon as she quits acting sore-footed. Shouldn't take too long, if you soak those front feet. But you'll have to go easy with her for quite a while. It's an awful strain on a horse's leg muscles and tendons, walking around on feet like that. You'll probably have to go slow and easy with her the rest of the summer."

Karen winced. All those Saddle Club trail rides...

After the veterinarian was gone Karen made herself a couple of sandwiches in her grandmother's kitchen and took them back to the pasture with her. She untied Lady Bay and led her slowly, gently, across the turnaround and into a lane leading between rows of high-fenced cattle pens. At the end of the lane was the calf pasture, where a score of curious yearlings watched their approach. Through the gate and across the pasture they went, slowly, painfully, scattering lizards and toads.

A gulch cut across the pasture. It was almost invisible from a distance, just a crack in the sandy ground. But looking down from its rim Karen and the mare saw the gulch filled almost to its brim with green, the dusty green of young willow trees. At the bottom a shallow stream lay waiting for them.

The downward trail had been beaten for them by generations of cattle coming to drink. The mare followed Karen easily enough down the slope and into the water, with only a brief pause while Karen kicked off her shoes. The water barely covered Karen's ankles but it was cool, shaded by the steep walls of the gulch and by the screen of willow saplings. As Lady Bay waded to a halt with the cool water swirling around her fetlocks she made a sound that seemed to Karen to be a groan of pleasure, or relief. The mare dropped her head, closed her eyes, relaxed her lower lip until it protruded ridiculously.

After a while Karen found a seat along the bank and ate her sandwiches. She leaned back on her elbows and luxuriated in the sight of her horse. It gave her intense pleasure to have relieved Lady Bay's pain by bringing her to the stream. She stared at the mare's head and tried to imagine the thoughts inside it.

Gratitude to her new owner? The beginning of love, or was it too soon after Cathy? Or did horses really love their owners, like dogs did?

"Are you still thinking about Cathy? Do you miss her still? It must have been something really special between the two of you, if she just got on and started riding you when you hadn't even been broken yet. I don't suppose anybody else will ever be that special to you. But I love you just as much as she did, don't you know that?"

The thought of Cathy and Lady Bay together brought a stomach-tightening mixture of emotions: jealousy that Lady Bay had loved another girl before her, a secret gladness that Cathy was dead and she was alive, shame at herself for being glad about anyone's death.

After a while, the temptation of her horse's back became too much for her, and Karen climbed on, using the bank as a mounting block. She watched closely for any sign that her weight was causing the mare pain, but Lady Bay dozed on, hardly seeming to notice the girl on her back.

Incredible elation filled Karen as she absorbed the feel of her horse. She stroked the mane, the neck, the warm place under the mane. She reveled in the curve of the barrel against her legs. After a while she carefully maneuvered herself until she was sitting backward, then she lay down, tenderly, with her cheek against the horse's croup, her arms lovingly encircling the hips. The fragrance of horse was strong, this close, and Karen closed her eyes to savor it.

They stayed in the stream most of the afternoon, until Karen grew aware of the time. This was sale night, maybe the night she would buy her bridle. Then, as soon as Lady's feet were well . . .

She smiled at the prospect of endless hours ahead

to be spent right here on this brown back. She turned around to riding position and pulled the lead rope, waking the mare and heading her up the slope. For the first few steps Karen tensed, watching and feeling for pain in the front hooves. There seemed to be none. Lady Bay climbed the gulch and ambled out across the pasture in steps that seemed normal to Karen.

"Cured? Already? Just one soak in the stream? I can't believe it. If I get a bridle tonight, and if you're not limping by tomorrow, we can go for a real ride. Wait till Grampa sees this."

But by the time they reached the yard, Lady Bay was showing signs of discomfort again in her front feet, and Karen was walking beside her.

"Oh well, that was too good to be true, I guess. But I'll be here tomorrow, and we'll soak your feet again, all day if we want to."

She gave her horse a measure of oats, a kiss on the nose, and a good-bye hug, then picked up her bike and pedaled home, hurrying now in case Harley came before she was ready.

✕ Eight ✕

What time was he supposed to pick you up?" Della asked. She was still at the supper table; Karen was leaning against the window frame in the built-on living room.

"It's usually around six-thirty."

"Is that when he said he'd pick you up?"

"Well, he didn't exactly say he was coming, but he always has been lately, on sale nights. I just expected him to, I guess." Karen's voice hit a forlorn note. "I was hoping to find a bridle, and they're probably selling the tack already, by now."

The kitchen clock said seven-fifteen.

Della stood up abruptly. "Come on, then, let's go."

"You'll take me?" Karen's voice was balanced between grateful relief and disappointment at spending sale night with her mother instead of Harley. But she lost little time in grabbing her purse and following her mother out to the Pinto.

The sale barn was outside of town on the highway, between the farm implement dealer and a sprawling truck stop. It was a ramshackle white barn surrounded by white plank holding pens, yellow now in the reflected sunset. In the parking area Harley's stock truck stood with the other trucks and trailers. The automatic joy Karen felt at the sight of his truck was tempered tonight by the weight of the question: Why hadn't he come for her?

She and Della went first to the sale ring within the barn. The ring was cluttered with miscellany, rope halters and lunging whips and a pony cart, a crate of half-grown rabbits and a half-dozen saddles new and used, and piles of horse blankets and saddle pads.

Karen picked her way through the stuff, searching for bridles. She found two that would do. The bidding was already underway. It went quickly and casually; the auctioneer was as eager as the sparse crowd to get through the cheap stuff and on to the animals.

Within a few minutes the auctioneer held up the better of the two bridles. It was dark with use, but the leather looked whole and healthy, and the bit looked good to Karen, not like the cheap aluminum one on the other bridle. The headstall was narrow with white stitching, just right for Lady Bay's head.

"Nice bridle here," the auctioneer swung it over his

head, "who'll give me two two two two, got it, give me five five five, four four—"

Karen raised her hand.

"Got it, five five five, gimme five five five. Y'all got your pockets sewed shut tonight, I see. Okay, hand up them saddle blankets, boys." He tossed the bridle to Karen.

"I got it?" she whispered to Della. "For four dollars?"

"Looks like. Take it back there, to the cashier, and pay for it."

Through her excitement over the bridle and her tension about Harley, it came to Karen that her mother was having fun. Together they bid several more times, and accumulated a rubber feed bucket, a rubber currycomb, a dandy brush with a varnished wood back, and a green-and-white lead rope. Della paid for most of it, and Karen paid for what she could, and they felt a closeness that was strange to both of them.

"Let's walk through the barns," Karen said. They put the bucket and other things in the car, but Karen hung the bridle around her neck and left it there. She liked the feel and the smell of it.

Behind the sale room stretched long aisles lined with pens for holding groups of horses. Karen saw the shape of her beloved Harley's back, far down the aisle, and she heard his laugh. She ran to him.

"Harley! Why didn't you come after me? I waited and—"

70

She stopped, realizing suddenly that she was interrupting a business talk. The potential customer was a woman, dark-haired, thin-lipped, her shirt tight. Harley's arm was around her shoulders.

" 'Scuse me for interrupting." Karen backed away a step. Her mother was coming slowly up the aisle, apparently absorbed in looking at the horses in the stalls.

"How are you this evening, Princess?" Harley said. To Karen's ears there seemed to be a forced quality to his cheer, as though he wished she'd go away. It was that way sometimes when he had to talk business. Karen understood.

"I just wanted to tell you," she said, "I got Lady Bay wormed today, and I soaked her feet for a long time and she was lots better after that. I don't think it's going to take very long at all, for her to get over the founder. I just love her."

She couldn't help seeing that arm of his. It had shifted up from the woman's shoulders to the plank of the pen behind them, but it still curved too close for Karen's comfort. She found herself wanting to be in the curve of that arm herself. She stared at the woman, and her look was colder than she knew.

Harley muttered, "Karen, this is a friend of mine. Lisa Lopez. Lisa, Karen."

The two nodded. Karen said stiffly to Harley, "Well, I just thought you'd want to know about Lady Bay."

She backed off till she felt her mother's touch. Della turned Karen with a casual supporting arm around her back, and said, "Come over here, honey. I want to show you something. Look. I bet it's not more than a month old. Isn't it darling?"

They peered through the slats into a pen that held a mare and her suckling foal. It was sufficient diversion for Karen's dignity to mend.

In the days that followed, Karen's absorption with her horse effectively blocked Harley from her thoughts. By the middle of the following week all the soreness was gone from Lady Bay's feet, and the long hours of soaking in the stream were finished. Mindful of leg muscles and tendons, Karen rode the mare gently over the soft sand of the pastures and across the broad, flat, mowed hay fields. July and August simmered slowly by, while the mare progressed from a stiff walk to a comfortable flowing lope.

With masses of roundworms expelled from her system Lady Bay began to absorb nourishment from the grain Karen fed her in careful amounts, and from the abundant pasture grass. She was still thin, but gaining, with just traces of rib shadows on her upper barrel, and only slightly pronounced hip bones. The daily brushing that gave equal pleasure to horse and girl began to raise a shine over shoulders and flanks.

Brushed and polished and loved, and wearing the white stitched bridle, Lady Bay was becoming a fair-looking horse. In a Saddle Club trail ride she would not have been one of the eye-catching horses, but neither would she have looked noticeably poorer than the average.

The summer trail rides came and went, but Karen let them pass. She was afraid of what a five-hour ride over rough country might do to Lady Bay's legs. And she had no way of transporting her horse to the starting point without calling Harley and asking for a ride. She could not bring herself to do that, although as the date for the first ride approached she carried the secret hope that he might call her and offer to take her. He didn't call, and she grimly closed her mind to him.

One day, shortly after she had begun to ride Lady Bay regularly, her grandfather said, "Did that fellow give you back half of what you paid him for that horse?"

"Harley?" Karen stalled. "Uh, yes, he did."

Willard nodded, satisfied. "Good. I just wanted to be sure. A hundred dollars isn't all that bad a price, I reckon, since she's not permanently crippled. But two hundred, that was robbery."

He went away talking to his dog, and Karen was left to wonder how Grampa had known about the refund. It sounded to her as though Grampa had talked to Harley about it, maybe even gotten mad at him and—

She didn't want to think that. Harley's generosity in reducing Lady Bay's price from four hundred to two was one of the best memories Karen had of him. It was right up there with the day he told her her mother loved her, and let her ride Sunny. She did not want to lose that bit of goodness from him.

So she rode, instead. She maneuvered Lady Bay around and among the yearling calves, playing cowboy with them but being careful not to get them running so that they would work off precious fat.

Laboriously she rolled three empty oil drums into a flat area in the pasture and set them up in a triangle, spaced properly for barrel-racing. She rode the pattern around the barrels as she remembered it from last summer's horse show, first at a slow jog, then faster as Lady Bay's legs healed, until they were doing the pattern at an easy lope with big cautious turns that would have earned them derisive laughter in any barrel race. But they enjoyed themselves.

Karen spent as many evenings as possible babysitting. There were shoes to buy, now that Lady Bay's hooves were back to normal. There was Grampa to be reimbursed for the vet bill, and the oats. There was a saddle to be saved for.

The second Sunday in August was the Sand Hills Saddle Club's annual show. Again, Karen hoped for a call from Harley, a breezy suggestion that she could ride along with him if she wanted. The call didn't come, and Karen suggested somewhat timidly to her mother that maybe the two of them could go. Della readily agreed, and Karen was startled at the pleasure she saw in her mother's eyes.

74

The club's arena was a simple affair, a large fenced oval set in a sparsely grassed plain. Along one side of the oval a sand hill rose steeply, and crude wooden bleachers climbed with it. The sky was brilliant turquoise over the rusty tints of the sand hills and the soft blues of distant mountains. Karen and Della sat high up in the bleachers, waving to friends, drinking cokes and watching the milling, sweat-shiny horses below.

As she watched the action inside the ring, Karen was always aware of the bright gold buckskin and his big handsome silver-haired rider. It made her chest ache to look directly at them, so she didn't do it very often.

During the gaming classes Karen concentrated on what was being done, and how. She memorized the barrel-racing pattern, and realized she and Lady Bay had been starting out in the wrong direction. She watched and studied, through reining classes and Stock Seat Equitation and Men's Western Pleasure. She expected to see Harley in that class, but the buckskin was not among the entrants.

So she was doubly surprised when Sunny entered with the next class, Ladies Western Pleasure. His rider was the dark-haired woman from the sale barn.

Karen excused herself and went to the rest room, and stayed till the class was over.

When she returned to Della in the bleachers the

Parade class was in the ring, seven big showy animals moving with arched necks under the weight of their silver-heavy trappings.

One of them was a palomino. Karen tensed. But this horse had high white stockings on all four legs; Galleon had had only low boots on the back legs.

"Do you think Galleon's still alive?" Karen ventured.

Della shrugged and said, "I suppose, but he'd be pretty old by now."

"I guess."

"Listen, kid," Della said brightly, "how about some good old rotten junk food?"

They got up and made their way down the bleachers and through the dust to the refreshment stand.

❧ Nine ❧

It was a Sunday afternoon in October. The cotton-
woods around the ranch house were in bright gold
leaf, dazzling against the rich blue of the sky. The day
was just cool enough to make the sun feel good; Willard and Etta shifted their lawn chairs away from the
shade. The day would have been a jewel of quiet
beauty except for the pen of newly weaned calves
beyond the barn, bellowing in high rage for their
mothers.

Karen stood at the pasture gate and watched as
her mother rode Lady Bay cautiously around the field.
At first she had been surprised at Della's awkward-
ness but when she'd had a few minutes to get used to
the idea, Karen found it endearing. It was somehow
easier to love a mother who was not in all ways
superior.

Horse and rider came back at an easy jog, a gait

that Karen could have sat without bouncing or clutch
ing Lady Bay's mane.

Della slid down and handed the reins to Karen.
"Whew, that's about enough for this old lady. Riding
bareback was never my specialty, and I haven't been
on a horse since before you were born. Oh, I'm going
to be so stiff tomorrow. But she's a very nice horse,
honey. Thank you for the ride."

Lady Bay rubbed her head against Karen's chest.

To her grandparents Karen said, "Anybody else
want to ride? Grampa? Want to try her out?"

He smiled, but shook his head and waved away
the suggestion.

"I'd like a little ride, if you please," Etta said, standing up resolutely. "If the rest of you think you can
boost me up. But, Karen, you hold on to her."

"You, Gramma?" Karen was delighted.

"Certainly, me. Lady Bay likes me. I give her my
apple cores."

"You'll get your slacks dirty," Della said, eyeing
her mother's neat turquoise pants and white blouse.

"That's all right. Everything's washable. Lead her
over here, Karen, by this stump. I think I can get on
from there."

With much laughter and boosting Etta was shoved
into place, and Karen led Lady Bay on a slow-motion
circle of the house. Safely back on her feet, Etta rewarded Lady Bay with a pat and an entire apple, and
Willard made caustic but good-natured remarks about

his wife's second childhood. Then he disappeared into the house and came back with the camera.

"Get back up on that horse, Mother. I want to record this for history."

While they were taking Gramma's picture, Della went inside and came back with a bit of green ribbon. "I found this in your sewing box, Mom. I hope you weren't going to use it for anything. Come here, Karen, I'll show you how I used to braid a ribbon into Galleon's mane. Here, you take this hunk of mane, right here behind the bridle. Hold that up at the top for me. That's it. Mom, we need the scissors. We've got enough ribbon left to do a braid in her forelock. You do that one, Karen."

When Lady Bay was braided and beribboned more pictures were taken, some with Karen astride, some with Karen standing close to the mare's head. Lady Bay, growing bored, rested her chin on Karen's shoulder and closed her eyes, and that instant, too, was caught by the camera.

On Thursday after school Karen picked up the photographs at the drugstore and ran all the way home to look at them in private. They were a feast for her eyes. She spread them on the kitchen table and lost herself in each of them, one at a time.

Her horse.

She picked up one of the pictures and looked at it more closely. The angle of horse to camera accentuated something Karen hadn't noticed before. Lady Bay was actually getting fat.

Karen whooped with pleasure, and made a decision. *This Saturday*, she thought, *I'm going to get her all brushed and braided up again, and ride her over to Harley's. I can hardly wait to show him how much she's changed. Show him what a good job I'm doing of taking care of her. He'll be so proud of me. And I can ask him about the saddle. Oh, I can hardly wait.*

At school on Friday she showed the pictures of her horse to two of her friendlier teachers, to the secretary in the school office, and to any of her friends who had ever expressed an interest in Lady Bay.

Friday night Karen washed her hair with Della's herbal shampoo that smelled so good.

She dreamed about Harley, a warm, confused dream that left her with a lovely afterglow in the morning.

It was a beauty of a day. They rode out in the morning sun, a brushed and shining girl on a brushed and shining brown mare. Karen rode gracefully erect, with an equestrian dignity unmarred by the canteen that hung from one side of her belt and the bag of sandwiches that hung from the other.

Following her grandfather's directions Karen rode diagonally across his fields and pastures, through obscure gates in the barbed-wire fences, and finally emerged on a dirt road leading toward the blacktop, and Harley's place. Crossing the fields they went at an easy jog, sometimes at a lope where the footing was good. They raised a spray of grasshoppers and toads, and now and then a jackrabbit.

On the road they went more slowly, and Karen could think of other things besides the joy of the ride. The stuff hanging from her belt reminded her of the saddle, which she could now afford if it wasn't new or expensive, and which she had not yet been able to find at the Friday night horse auctions in Sand Hills.

"He'll be able to find me one," she said aloud, and the mare's ears flicked back to catch the sound. "As many sales as he goes to, he shouldn't have any trouble finding me a nice little single-rig saddle, not too big and heavy. A black one, with a little carving here and there. Nice padded seat. Maybe a matching breastplate if it didn't cost too much. And then when I get some more money, I can get saddlebags to carry my food in when we go for long rides. Wouldn't that be fun?"

A little later another idea occurred to her. "I'm going to ask him for the name and address of Cathy's parents. I'm going to send them one of those pictures, and show them what a good home you have now. That should make them feel good. It might make them a little bit ashamed of themselves, too, for letting you get in such bad shape." She stroked the mare's neck.

She was relieved to see Harley's truck parked near the corral when the ranch came into view. By now her anticipation at seeing him again was painfully keen. It had been two months since she had watched him from the bleachers at the horse show, and that hardly counted because they hadn't talked. And before that, the meeting at the sale barn had been spoiled by that Lisa. Since then, there had been no contact between them.

My fault, Karen thought. *I've been out at Grampa's every weekend, riding Lady Bay, instead of coming out here like I used to on Saturdays during school. He probably thinks I don't like him anymore. Maybe he even thinks I was just hanging around him till he got my horse for me, and then I dropped him because I didn't have any use for him anymore. He couldn't have thought that. Could he? Maybe I did hurt his feelings. Maybe that was why he wasn't very friendly that night at the sale barn. And at the horse show, when we waved at him, and he waved back but didn't come over and talk like he would have before.*

She rode up the farm lane, bursting with determination to assure Harley that their very special friendship was just as strong as ever.

"Harley!" she yelled.

He wasn't in sight. She slipped down and tied Lady Bay to Harley's truck, on the shady side.

"Harley? Where are you hiding?"

She looked over the corral fence. No one there but horses. The interior of the barn was dark and quiet and empty.

"That's funny," Karen mused. She looked around, frowning. The only place left was the house. But Harley seldom went in there. It was little and falling apart and empty, and it smelled of snakes inside. He had showed it to her once, long ago. There was nothing in there but a ratty old chair and a mattress understandably left behind by whoever had lived there last. So he couldn't be in the house.

"He must be out riding someplace on one of the horses," she told Lady Bay. "We'll just make ourselves comfortable here, and wait for him. He probably won't be gone very long."

She settled herself behind the truck and opened her sandwich bag.

"It's okay, she's—" Harley's voice, from the door of the house. Karen looked around the end of the truck and impaled him on her stare.

"Where were you? I was looking all over for you. Didn't you hear me yelling? What were you—"

Karen's voice faded. There was someone in the house with Harley. Karen could see no one, hear no one, but she knew. There was a woman in there. The flush on his face, the movement of his eyes, told her so.

As he walked toward her Harley smiled, collected himself. "I didn't hear you. What are you doing out here?" His tone was affable, but didn't seem genuine to Karen.

Stiffly she said, "I wanted to show you how Lady Bay was coming along. I thought you'd be interested, since she was so special to you, because of Cathy and all that."

He walked around the truck and glanced at the

83

mare. "She's looking good, honey. You're taking good care of her, all right." But he wasn't really looking.

In an oddly formal voice Karen went on. "I had a couple of other things I wanted to talk to you about, too. I wanted to get the name and address of Cathy's parents, so I could send them a picture of Lady Bay. I thought they'd like to see that their daughter's horse got a good home."

"I don't know if I've got it," Harley said, somewhat hastily. "I'll check around in my records at home, see if I've got it there."

"Will you call me when you find it?"

"Sure."

"Promise?"

"I promise. Was there something else you wanted?"

He was trying to get rid of her. Karen ached.

"I was wondering if you'd look for a saddle for me," she said stiffly. "I've got fifty dollars saved up. I've been looking for one around here, but I can't find what I want. I want a smallish one, not too heavy, a single-rig with a padded seat, a black one if possible, and I'd like leather-covered stirrups but that's not too important."

"Sure, I'll keep my eye out."

Deep inside Karen's jeans pocket was the wad of bills, two months' worth of baby-sitting money. She started to fish it out, but some instinct stilled her hand.

"If you find one like that, get it for me and I'll pay you back, but fifty dollars is my limit."

She untied her mare and jumped up onto her back. Without looking at Harley, she reined away and loped toward the blacktop, hoping viciously that Harley felt as rotten as she did.

Her anger carried her along the blacktop, along the dirt road shortcut, and into the far fields of her grandfather's land. But, dismounting to open a wire gate, she gave in to the temptation of Lady Bay's neck, and cried into the black strands of her friend's mane.

Mounted again, sniffing, Karen tried to sort out her hurts. *So what if he has some woman out there?* she told herself. *That shouldn't be any big surprise to me by now, that Harley likes women, that he's maybe not a hundred percent faithful to his wife. So why should that bother me? I probably shouldn't have come barging in like that. But heck, I've been out there a hundred times on Saturdays. He's always been glad to see me before, or at least he never acted like he wanted to get rid of me.*

She rode slowly now, pondering, replaying the scene, re-probing her hurts. Yet she carefully avoided any recognition of the possibility that she was jealous.

✖ Ten ✖

The next morning Lady Bay was foundered again.

Karen arrived at mid-morning, prepared for an all-day ride to ease the hurts of yesterday. She found the mare standing in the pasture, head down, back humped, hind legs drawn forward to take the painful weight off of her inflamed front feet.

"Oh, no," Karen wailed. She ran forward and grasped Lady Bay's front leg at the knee. The mare tried to yield her foot, but winced and whistled in extreme pain as her weight shifted to her other forefoot.

Tears made clean streaks in the road-dust on Karen's face as she tried to lead Lady Bay toward the pasture gate, toward the distant stream in the calf pasture. The mare tried to follow, but her movements were so halting, so painful, that Karen stopped near the gate and released the halter.

"You wait here, sweetheart."

She ran to the barn and came back with two rubber feed buckets filled with icy water from the barn pump. Carefully she placed them before the inflamed hooves.

"No, don't drink. I'll bring you another bucket to drink. These are for your feet. Here. Like this."

She lifted one black leg and eased the hoof into the bucket. As she reached for the other leg, Lady Bay lifted it herself and set it, sighing, in the bucket. Karen left the mare and ran to the house.

Her grandparents were at church. The house was Sunday still and tidy, and the dinner roast was simmering in a slow oven. Its fragrance nauseated Karen as she fumbled through the phone book for the veterinarian's number.

He was sympathetic and soothing, but said there was little he could do. "If it will make you feel any better, I'll stop out after a while and take a look at her, but if you've got her feet soaking, that's about all anybody can do for her at this point."

By the time he arrived, two hours later, Karen's agitation was near the boil-over point.

"What happened to her? What did I do wrong? I didn't water her when she was hot. I was very careful about that. I rode her about five miles yesterday, but not fast, honestly. And most of it was on grass. Would that have done it? I haven't been giving her any grain at all lately, because she's getting so fat."

He shook his head. "I wouldn't think a five-mile

ride on soft ground should hurt her. She'd gotten over that last attack. But it might have. You just can't tell with this chronic founder. It can flare up just about any time, seems like. It probably wasn't anything you did at all."

Karen wailed, "But if I don't know what I did to cause another attack, how can I keep from doing it again? I thought when she got over that other attack that she was cured, and I wouldn't have to worry about her anymore. Now this— is it going to go on like this all her life? Won't I ever be able to ride her like a normal horse?"

He gripped her shoulder with a steadying hand. "I just can't say, Karen. You've taken awful good care of this mare. She's a different animal from what you started out with. If I was you I believe I'd sell her when she gets on her feet again, and get a good sound horse that you can enjoy. You deserve it. And next time I'd steer clear of any dealings with Harley Williams."

The tears began again. "I could never sell Lady Bay. I love her."

The doctor looked away, embarrassed, and ran his hand over Lady Bay's back and hips. "Well," he said more cheerfully, "one good thing about it. Her colt's not likely to inherit the problem."

Karen was thunderstruck.

"Her *what*?"

He glanced at her, over his shoulder. "The mare is

in foal, isn't she?" He brushed the full brown flank with his fingertips.

"Not that I know of," Karen sputtered. "He would have told me—the people that owned her would have told Harley when he bought her, wouldn't they? It would make her more valuable if she was going to have a colt. And he would have told me. If he knew about it. But maybe—do you think—is she really?"

A sunburst of glory exploded in Karen's head.

"I don't know," the doctor said, "that might just be a hay belly on her, but it feels pretty solid to me. I can check her and find out for sure."

Karen glowed at him. He went to his truck and came back with a very long transparent plastic glove, and antiseptic lubricant. He rolled up his sleeve and slipped on the glove.

"You talk to her a little bit, while I go in. I don't think we'll need to put a twitch on her to distract her. She's too sore to kick me."

He lifted her tail and inserted his arm, almost to the shoulder. Karen stared at his face, longing to read affirmation in his expression.

He grinned and withdrew his plastic-coated arm. "Somebody in there, all right."

"She's really going to have a colt? I can't believe it. Oh, thank you, thank you, thank you!" She hugged first the mare, then the veterinarian.

He laughed. "Don't thank me. I had nothing to do with it."

Karen laughed. She couldn't stop herself. "And here I've been cutting back on her feed, thinking she was just fat. Stupid, stupid, why didn't I think! When is it going to be born?"

"Well, it felt like about a six-month fetus in there, that'd mean it was probably conceived around April, May. That'll give you an early spring foal, some time around March, most likely."

"Oh, I can't wait, I can't wait." Karen bounced on her toes, and hugged herself. "Tell me everything I should be doing. Should I be feeding her oats again? Should I keep worming her? Can I keep riding her when her feet get better?"

She followed him to his truck.

"I'd ease her back up to maybe four, five quarts of grain a day, but do it gradually. See that she's got her fill of hay or good pasture. We'll give her one more worming after frost, to get the bots out of her system. And I'll give you a vitamin supplement, since she was in poor condition early in the pregnancy. Ride her gently, like you have been, but don't let her do any sudden turns or stops, anything like that."

Karen was still caroling her thanks as he drove away. She ran back to feel Lady Bay's belly, searching for a bump that might be the baby. Then she ran, whooping and leaping, toward the house to tell her grandparents the wonderful news.

At first, the news of the coming foal was enough to keep Karen inflated with a happiness that filled her mind and left only enough room around the edges for necessary schoolwork and the chores of daily living.

She lived in a continual daydream with her colt. He was her horse from the instant of his birth and he grew, in her fantasy, through all the endearing stages of colthood into a mature and beautiful animal whose mind and will were tuned to hers. A horse that no one but Karen Kohler was ever allowed to ride; a horse who allowed no other rider.

Her fantasies included scenes in which she led her gleaming, prancing yearling through halter class competition at the Sand Hills horse show; scenes in which she and her horse came away victorious in the Ladies Western Pleasure class, and the Barrel Race. And admiring little girls came to stroke his shoulder and say where did you get that beautiful horse, can I ride him, and Karen answered, kindly, that she couldn't give them rides because this horse wouldn't carry anyone but her, she'd raised him from a colt, you see, and no one else had ever been on him.

But eventually the daydreams wore thin, and Karen's mind turned toward the reality of her colt.

She knew nothing of the stallion who had sired the foal within Lady Bay.

"You ought to try to find out," Della said one evening at the supper table. "For all you know the stud might be a purebred something or other. Quarter horse maybe, or Arab. If it was an Arab and you had proof of the breeding, you could register the colt in the Half-Arab Registry. Or it might be a Paint, or an Appaloosa."

"I know it," Karen said. "I've been thinking that same thing myself."

"Well?"

"Well what?"

"Why aren't you doing something about it? Get hold of Harley and find out if he knows anything about it. He could at least give you the name and address of the people he bought Lady Bay from, and you could write to them."

Karen was silent. She had been thinking these very thoughts for several days now, but she didn't know how to approach Harley. Biking out to his farm on a weekend was out of the question. Absolutely. The humiliation of her last visit there precluded that possibility. She couldn't quite bring herself to go to his apartment, and she didn't want to do it over the phone.

She wanted to see him again.

She ached to see him again, because an achingly optimistic thought had come to her a few days ago. Harley must have known that Lady Bay was bred. He must have decided not to tell Karen, in case something went wrong and the breeding didn't take. Karen knew from her reading that mares frequently fail to conceive after being bred, or else they abort during the early weeks of the pregnancy. The more Karen thought about it, the more logical it seemed to her. It would explain the four hundred-dollar price, which was not an unfair price for an in-foal mare, especially if she were bred to a good, purebred stallion. And it would be in keeping with the gentle thoughtfulness that Harley used to show Karen, if he had decided not to tell her about the foal until it was a sure thing.

It would mean that she was special to him, even though they hadn't seen much of each other lately, even though she had irritated him by showing up at the ranch at an awkward time.

This newly reborn feeling for Harley made Karen want to talk to him in person. Lady Bay's pregnancy was a legitimate bit of business to discuss with him, a genuine reason to seek him out. She didn't want to squander it by phoning.

She wanted to see him, and hear his voice, and get a big warm shoulder-hug.

"Why don't you call him?" Della persisted.

Karen could think of no plausible excuse. Della's suggestion was the logical thing to do. Call him up and ask him about the stallion.

"Go on, honey. I'm curious to find out, myself." Della smiled and nudged Karen's leg with the toe of her loafer.

Karen sighed and got up. No way out of it. She dialed Harley's number.

Mrs. Williams answered. "He's not here. I expect he's down at the bar, but he don't usually stay too awful late. Want me to have him call you?"

"Yes, please. Tell him it's important. Tell him it's good news, okay?"

"You bet."

But he didn't call. Not that night, nor the next nor the next.

With each day Karen grew more grim, more secretly fearful, more anxious to see him and get it over with.

Finally, after school one afternoon, she gathered her determination around her and went into Gloria's Kut and Kurl Shoppe, in the less desirable of the two downtown blocks.

There was only one operator in the shop, a brittle blond woman whose hair looked several years too young for her face.

"Are you Mrs. Williams?" Karen asked.

"That's right, honey. Whatcha' need? Cut and perm?"

"No, I'm Karen Kohler. I've been trying to get hold of Harley. You remember, I called the other night and he was supposed to—"

"Didn't he call you back? He probably forgot. He's upstairs. Go out that door and up the stairs, first door on the right. Bang loud, honey, he's probably asleep."

Her heart thudded noticeably as Karen climbed the stairway. *That's silly*, she told herself. *I'm just going to talk business. I have every right. No reason to feel nervous, it's just my same old Harley.*

When he answered her knock he seemed fuzzy-minded, as though for an instant he didn't recognize her.

"Can I talk to you for a minute, Harley?"

94

"Oh. Karen. What are you doing here? Sure, come in. I was just catching up on my sleep. Been away on a buying trip, drove all night."

Karen was instantly contrite. "Oh, I'm sorry. I shouldn't have come. You probably need your sleep. Do you want me to go away and come back later?"

He yawned and scratched, and sat astride a chair arm, leaving Karen to stand awkwardly in the middle of the cluttered room.

"No, that's okay. What's your problem?"

She took a deep breath. "It's not a problem, it's wonderful news. Lady Bay is going to have a colt. You knew about it, didn't you? I bet you didn't want me to be disappointed if it didn't work out, so you didn't tell me when I bought her, huh?"

"Uh," he rubbed his head. "That's good news. A colt will be nice for you. Well, if you'll excuse me, I got to get—"

"No, wait. What I came for was, I need to find out about the stallion, the colt's sire. Do you know anything about him, what kind he was or anything like that?"

"No, honey, I don't know nothing about that, sorry." He stood, and Karen knew, with a sinking certainty, that he wanted to be rid of her.

"Well, at least can you give me the name and address of the family you bought her from, so I can write them and ask them?"

"Family?"

"Cathy's family. You know." Karen stared hard at

him. "You know, Cathy, the girl who died. You told me—"

The room grew silent.

Karen stared at Harley, and his eyes moved away from her gaze, off to the side.

She knew, then.

In a quiet voice, threaded with pain, Karen said, "There wasn't any Cathy, was there? You made that all up, that whole story. Just to sell me a horse. Just to get more money out of me. You were afraid I wouldn't be sucker enough to buy a thin old foundered horse, so you made up that story so I'd feel sorry for her, and buy her. So you'd have an excuse to charge me four hundred dollars."

He forced a smile, and reached out to pat her arm. "Now listen, honey, you like the little mare, don't you? What difference does it make—"

But Karen was gone, running.

❧ Eleven ❧

Winter closed in on Sand Hills, bringing snow that blew across the flatlands, leaving open fields nearly bare but drifting high over fences and low-roofed sheds. During an especially vicious ice storm several head of Willard Kohler's cattle smothered to death when ice enclosed their nostrils. On larger ranches, isolated herds were fed by helicopter hay-drops.

Lady Bay spent her nights in a sheltered corner of Willard's main barn, and her days picking her way across the frozen ground of the adjoining lot, which she shared with twenty-seven stock cows who were also pregnant. Willard gave the mare her morning feeding, and often stopped for a word or two with her.

On days when the driving conditions were not too dangerous, Della and Karen drove out after five, through gentle blue twilights, so that Karen could do the evening feeding and visit Lady Bay, and hold her palm against the increasingly full brown flanks that held the foal. Occasionally on a weekend the weather and the footing allowed for a little bit of riding, and Karen settled herself with relish deep in the wool of the mare's winter coat.

During those weeks Karen strained to focus her thoughts on anything but Harley Williams. She had an unusually disciplined mind for her age, and for moderately long periods of time she was able to keep from thinking about him. The coming foal helped greatly.

But there were times when her bereavement engulfed her. She lay in bed, after the trailer was quiet and dark, and listened to country music on her radio, and cried. The less she thought about him during the day, the more persistent were her dreams about him at night.

"It was just a silly crush," she repeated silently into her pillow, her jaws clenched hard against the swelling ache in her throat. "I had a crush on him. He was probably a father figure or some stupid thing like that. Only it wasn't real. I didn't know him, as he really is, I was just in love with my idea of him. What I wanted him to be."

The words, the knowledge, did nothing to soothe the bruised emptiness in her, where her love for Harley had been all these years.

Della didn't know, and that helped. When she was

with her mother, Karen was forced to act normally, and the act gradually tended to become reality.

Early in February Della completed her correspondence course and passed the Allied Mutual Insurance examination. She hired a secretary to replace herself, and moved into a tiny back office to become a fully accredited salesperson.

When her first enlarged paycheck arrived, Della and Karen dressed up and went out to the Country Inn Steak House at the edge of town and ordered the biggest New York Sirloin on the menu.

It was a gala meal.

"You know where sirloins got their name?" Della said, gesturing with her fork. "This is no lie. I read it someplace. King Henry the Eighth declared that loin of beef was such a magnificent dish that he knighted it."

"You're kidding," Karen laughed. "You made that up."

"No, honest. He dubbed it Sir Loin. Gave it a whack with his sword, the whole shootin' match."

They laughed together, and Karen said, "If you're not going to finish your Sir Salad, pass it over here. My Lady Cole Slaw is all gone."

When the fun and the food were finished, Karen leaned back and said, "That was good, Mom. Thanks. I could get used to that kind of a meal."

Della wadded up her napkin and peeked at the check. "Well, we're not going to be living this high on the hog every night, but I'd say things are going to be looking up from now on. I was thinking . . ." She paused.

"What, what?"

"Well, a couple of things. Not for sure yet, but it looks like the budget is going to be able to handle a little better car for me, in a few months. Then when you get your license you could have the Pinto. It's paid for, and it's not worth much as a trade-in. It'd get you back and forth to the farm, anyway."

Karen's eyes widened. "Mom. You mean it? Really?"

"Don't screech in a public place. And the other thing I've been thinking about, well, for a long time I've been wishing we could sell the trailer and get us a nice little house. I get so sick of frozen water pipes in the winter, and worrying about tornados in the summer."

Karen was bouncing on her seat. "In the country? At least an acreage at the edge of town where I could have the horses?"

"Well, if we could find something we liked, and if it was within our budget, and if we could find a buyer for the trailer. At any rate we can kind of keep our eyes open."

For Karen it was almost too many good prospects at once. Her daydreaming centered on the foal, the house in the country, the freedom of a car and driver's license. Less and less frequently did the country music make her cry in the late-night darkness of her bedroom.

The process of forgetting Harley was coming along

100

nicely within Karen until one morning late in February.

Karen and Della were in the kitchen, Karen watching the eggs cooking in the skillet and Della moving from refrigerator to toaster to table, assembling breakfast. Both were in robes and slippers and warm, long-legged pajamas. There was always a draft along the trailer floor in cold weather. Neither of them had begun talking yet, beyond monosyllables and pre-verbal sounds. They were both slow starters early in the morning.

The little plastic radio on top of the refrigerator was tuned to the Fort Morgan station, which was as close as Sand Hills came to local radio.

"If you liked yesterday's weather," the announcer said, "you're going to love today's. More of the same, folks, cloudy, chance of light snow by afternoon, highs expected to be in the upper teens, lows near zero. Winds twenty to thirty miles per, so button up those overcoats, friends and sweethearts."

"I wish he'd give the news and cut the funny stuff," Della groused. "It's too early in the morning for all—"

"Shh." Karen waved her mother silent.

The radio said, ". . . shooting incident reported last night. Authorities at Sand Hills say the shooting took place in an abandoned ranch house owned by Ervin Carlisle, three miles south of Sand Hills. Injured were fifty-three-year-old Harley Williams, who leased the property, and twenty-year-old Lisa Lopez of the same city."

Karen stared, slack-jawed, at Della who froze in position, reaching for the toast. The eggs in the skillet turned brown at the edges, unnoticed.

The radio went on. "Mr. Williams escaped with minor injuries. Miss Lopez is hospitalized in fair condition, suffering from gunshot wounds in the chest and shoulder."

The announcer moved on to other stories, and Karen threw out the ruined eggs and started two new ones, but her movements were automatic. Her mind was on Harley.

"I can't believe it. Harley, shot. It's awful. I wonder if he's hurt bad."

Della settled herself at the table and began to eat. "Minor injuries, he said. Probably caught a little buckshot around the edges. I wouldn't waste your sympathy on him, if I were you. Matter of fact, I think it's kind of fitting. He's been playing cowboy all his life. A shoot-out'll be just the ticket for him. Although I must say the circumstances are not exactly dignified, here. Oh well, by the time ole Harley gets through doctoring up the story, he's going to come off like John Wayne. The one you ought to feel sorry for is that woman. Gunshot wounds in the chest and shoulder. That could have been fatal. Whew. Wouldn't wish that on anybody, even on somebody dumb enough to get herself involved with Harley Williams."

She glanced at Karen's face, then patted her daughter on the arm. "I'm sorry, honey, I know he used to be your friend. People can act differently with different people, after all. I mean, you were a little kid without a daddy, and he was nice to you. And that's all well and good. I'm just glad you got shut of him when you did. You're getting up to an age now where running around with Harley Williams could hurt your reputation. Especially after something like this."

Karen dropped her eyes, and ate a few bites. She wasn't hungry, but it was easier to eat than to fight her mother's pressure to do so. And she didn't want Della to know that Harley still had the power to churn her stomach like this.

"I wonder who did it," Karen said. "The shooting."

"Woman's husband, no doubt, or boyfriend or whatever."

She was almost finished with breakfast before it occurred to Karen. "That's funny, he told me he owned that place. He used to tell me all about this house he wanted to build out there, this big log ranch house with stone fireplaces and all that. And all he was doing was renting the pasture for his horses." She shook her head.

Della stood and picked up her coffee cup. Passing Karen, she stroked her head. "Hon, there are just some people in the world that you can't believe a blessed blue-eyed thing they tell you. And Harley Williams is sure as heck one of them."

In a town like Sand Hills, a dramatic act of violence occurred so rarely that it became the major topic of conversation on every level of society, from the board meeting at the bank to the elementary school playground at recess. By the end of the day, all the details had spread from the hospital and police stations to almost every ear in town.

In most opinions, there were three equally guilty parties: Danny Fischer, who had done the shooting and who was being referred to by the news media as Lisa's common-law husband; Lisa for being unfaithful to Danny and foolish enough to get herself into that situation with a man like Harley; and Harley himself for messing around behind his wife's back with a girl young enough to be his daughter.

At first, whatever sympathy there was was aimed at Lisa because of her injuries, and at Harley's wife, whom most of the women in town knew and liked. Gloria did a nice tint job, she could give a permanent without frizzing it up, and her prices were right. Furthermore, Gloria Williams was always cheerful, always willing to pass the time of day with her customers, enjoyed an occasional bit of gossip but never in a spiteful way. She supported a husband who was a lazy good-for-nothing even though he was a good-looking fellow, and pleasant enough, but everybody knew it was Gloria who paid the bills, and he couldn't be much of a man if he'd let her do that, year after year.

After a few days Lisa was released from the hospital, Danny was tucked away in the county jail, and Gloria's customers began to overcome their shyness and keep their hair appointments. The incident was still talked about some, but it lost precedence to other matters.

For Karen, nothing was as important as the coming foal, not even Harley.

✖ Twelve ✖

The call came at a little after six, on the morning of March eleventh.

"Karen? This is Grampa. Got a little surprise for you, you better come out and have a look."

Della was emerging from her room, staggering slightly, as Karen hung up the phone.

"The colt's born, the colt's born! Hurry up, get dressed, hurry, hurry." Karen was already flinging on her jeans and sweat shirt.

"Boy or girl?" Della asked.

"I don't know. I didn't take time to ask. Hurry, Mom. We can eat breakfast out there. Come on, I'm ready. Let's go."

She ran to the car and stood, bouncing on her toes while Della fumbled for the key. The car stalled twice before it was on the street and moving.

"Can't you drive a little faster?" Karen leaned

forward against the Pinto's dashboard, pushing the car along the highway.

"Not without getting arrested," Della said drily. "And believe me, I'm in as much of a hurry as you are. You didn't give me time to go to the bathroom even."

"You can do that when we get there. First things first."

Before the car was fully stopped, Karen was out and running.

Willard and Etta stood in the frame of the barn door, smiling. Karen ran toward them.

"Is it alive and healthy?"

"Fine as frog's hair," Willard said, and stepped aside.

Mare and foal stood in their partitioned-off corner of the big, dim cow barn. The light wasn't good in that corner, but the foal seemed to radiate his own glow.

He was pale cream, fading to white on his legs. His eyes were huge and dark and curious as he peered at Karen. His coat was still a bit damp and wavy, and drops of dark red fell slowly from the few inches of umbilical stump.

"He's bleeding," Karen whispered, alarmed.

Her grandfather laughed. "That's iodine. I just got through painting the stump, so it doesn't get infected. It's a fine colt, Karen, big and strong and healthy. He was up nursing by the time I found him, and he was still wringing wet so he must have been just born."

Karen went into the stall and stared, with awe, at the baby horse. She felt sniffly with the beauty of the miracle, but didn't want to cry in front of Grampa. She stroked Lady Bay's sweat-dampened neck and murmured, "Thank you."

She reached toward the foal and brushed his rump with her fingertips. He continued to nurse for a few more minutes, weaving on his propped-up legs. Then, almost without warning, his eyelids drooped and he collapsed into the straw. He was asleep. The mare shifted so that she could hang her head over him, blowing gently and licking now and then.

Della came into the barn, delayed by her side trip to the house. Willard left to finish his morning chores, and Etta returned to her kitchen, and breakfast. Karen raised her finger to her lips, smiled, and motioned for Della to look.

"It's a palomino," Della said. "Or is it?"

Karen nodded. "That's the color they are when they're born," she said. "He'll turn darker. Probably. Just like Galleon."

Just like Galleon, Karen thought. *She gave up Galleon for me. And now, here he is back again.*

Before she could think through her impulse, and weaken, Karen turned to her mother. It was clear what she had to do.

"He belongs to you, Mom."

Della stared. "What are you talking about?"

"I'm giving him to you. It was my fault you lost Galleon, so now I'm making it up to you. He's—well, don't cry. Don't, Mom."

Della turned away, her shoulders humping with

108

sobs. In a minute she caught her breath and groped for a Kleenex in her coat pocket.

She gathered her daughter in her arms in an awkward hug. "Honey, you could never in your life give me anything that'd mean more to me than that offer. But I could never take your colt. He belongs to you, and that's the way it's supposed to be. But—thank you."

Karen's relief choked the words in her throat. She could only nod against her mother's coat collar.

"Come on now," Della said briskly, "your Gramma's waiting breakfast, and then we've got to get back to town. You've got school, and I've got work. Lady Bay can take care of everything here till this evening."

Della sat in the trailer kitchen. Karen had left for school, and there was just time for a cup of coffee before Della was due at the office. She sat blank-faced, her fingers curled around a coffee mug that was cooling unnoticed.

Della's eyes were focused not on the kitchen but on Jim Tucker, on Tucker's face in that crowded little pickup camper at the Cheyenne Rodeo Grounds. It was a hot August night, and the camper door and windows were open to the breeze and the noise from other rigs parked nearby.

It was late, well after midnight. The evening's performance was finished and the crowd was gone. Only the rodeoers were left, drinking and whooping and partying from trailer to camper to corrals, celebrating the day's winnings or laughing off the defeats and injuries.

Tucker was one of the startlingly handsome young men who seemd to be more the rule than the exception on the rodeo circuit. His features were a charming mixture of boyish curves and masculine angles.

He even managed to look smooth and self-possessed as he said, "Listen, Sugar, if you were careless enough to get yourself in that kind of fix, it's too bad, but it ain't no skin off my nose. Now, you knew all along that I wasn't the marrying kind. You got no call to try to trap me now, with—this is the oldest trick in the book, you know that? You're probably not even pregnant. Or if you are, it's probably not mine. I want you out of here, you and that horse of yours. I'm tired of hauling the both of you around. I'm going out for a little drink with my friends, and when I get back I want you gone. Understand?"

Gone. Easy for him to say. Della was furious enough to wish herself a million miles away, but it wasn't that simple. She was far from home, she had no money, she had a horse to transport, so she couldn't hitchhike home. For that matter, she had no home, no parents willing to take back a daughter who had run away from them, with a guy they had warned her against, and had gotten herself pregnant.

One possibility did occur to her, as she slammed her few belongings into her small suitcase. Harley Williams, if he was still here. She looked out the camper door and saw Harley's stock truck still parked where it had been all day. With a frantic sense of hope Della ran toward it. Her mind was muddled. She didn't know what to ask Harley, she only knew that he was a friend, he liked her, he was from home, he had a stock truck, he bought horses. . . .

Harley was seated a little distance from his truck, in a circle of laughing, lounging men and women gathered around an ice chest full of beer cans.

"Can I talk to you for a minute?" Della said.

"Sure, honey. Have a beer. Where's Tuck at?"

"No, thanks. Harley, I need to talk to you alone."

They left the others and settled in the cab of Harley's truck.

"I'm in trouble," Della said abruptly.

"*Trouble* trouble?"

She sighed and nodded. "Tuck kicked me out. I guess he doesn't want a pregnant playmate. And," she drew a ragged breath. "I don't have a cent of money. And I can't go home this way. Can you think of anything . . ."

Harley frowned and rubbed his beer can over the crest of the steering wheel. "That horse belong to you?"

"Yes."

"Tell you what. I'll stretch my usual limits a little. Give you, say, five hundred for him. That'll be enough to get you a little operation, enough to get you home afterward. Or if you want to catch up with Tuck at Sioux Falls, you could probably get back in his good books again, if you tried."

"Like hell," Della said through clenched teeth.

"Well, at least you could go home to your folks, and they'd never need to know about it."

Della was silent. It wasn't the first time, these past weeks, that the possibility of an abortion had occurred to her. She didn't like the idea. It scared her. It terrified her, but so did the prospect of facing her parents, of going through a birth, of raising a child by herself. The only happy alternative would have been for Tuck to marry her, if only briefly. But...

She sighed.

Harley said, "I can give you the name of a place you can go, here in Cheyenne. They'll do a good job and I don't think they charge more than two, three hundred. It's your best bet, hon."

Harley seemed so mature, so experienced, so sure. After a few minutes Della nodded.

She accepted the name and address that he wrote on the back of a feed store receipt. She accepted the five hundred dollars, and she led Galleon from Tucker's four-horse trailer to Harley's truck. She opened the tack bin in the front of Tuck's trailer, pondered the silver mounted saddle which was worth at least as much as the horse. It would be easy enough to sell, even tonight, in a crowd like this. But it belonged to Tuck.

She picked up the matching bridle. A hundred-and-fifty-dollar bridle, any day.

"He owes me that," she muttered, and jammed the bridle into her suitcase.

She went through the horror of the abortion and came out water-weak, and sick, and five hundred dollars poorer—and, by fluke, still pregnant.

But she was too tired to fight it any longer. She hitched home to Sand Hills.

Della sat in the trailer kitchen with her chilled coffee mug, and pondered on how little she deserved her daughter.

✣ Thirteen ✣

For several weeks after the shooting Harley stuck close to the apartment when he wasn't out of town on a buying trip. But eventually his gregarious nature pushed him into Max's. It was a Friday night, payday at the packing plant, and the place was full.

A slight but noticeable silence followed Harley through the room and up to the bar.

"Howdy Max, pull me a draft, will you?"

The talk around him resumed. Max served him and smiled, but didn't stay to visit.

He turned to the woman on the stool beside him. "Hi there, sweet stuff."

She gave him a quick cool smile, and resumed her conversation with the man on her other side.

Harley looked slowly around the room, searching for eyes to meet, friends to greet. They all seemed absorbed in one another. For the first time in his memory, Harley felt the chill of isolation.

The band struck up "Your Cheatin' Heart," and they grinned at Harley as they always had, but there was no one interested in listening to the story about Hank Williams being Harley's uncle.

Eventually a tableful of men waved at Harley to join them, and he did, and was absorbed easily enough into the group. But after that Harley began doing his drinking at home, evenings.

And even home wasn't what it used to be. The publicity of the shooting had brought Gloria more humiliation than even her placid temperament was capable of accepting. Their relationship became almost like that of a landlady and a boarder, a boarder who was behind in his payments. They shared the apartment, but nothing more.

Lisa was gone, of course.

The horse-crazy teenage girls had all been warned away from Harley Williams, so he no longer had the pleasure of those flirtations. And the women in Max's, when he did go in, no longer looked at him warmly, or listened when he talked. They all knew who he was, and they all carried painfully clear mental images of Lisa Lopez, shot full of holes.

As the spring progressed Harley found himself remembering more and more often the little Kohler girl. With a soft smile he recalled how she used to look up at him with that worshiping expression. How she used to ride that bike of hers all the way out to the ranch, on a Saturday, just to be in his company.

He remembered how damn awful good it had been, having somebody who looked up to him that way.

It was a Saturday afternoon in May, a sparkler of a day, brilliant turquoise sky, fresh-washed grass, and the tamerisk around the farmhouse covered with bright pink blossoms. A light wind snapped the washing on Etta's clothesline. She had a perfectly good dryer in the basement, Sears' best, bought at her employee's discount, but it would have been close to sinful not to dry outdoors on a day like this.

Inside the barn Karen bent and puffed and sweated, her lips clamped over a row of nails. It was beginning to shape up. She finished nailing the last two little boards and stood back to look at it. It was a saddle rack, built out from a bare bit of plank wall near the horses' stall.

"I believe that does it," she said aloud. She picked up her saddle and set it carefully on the rack. Nothing broke. She grinned and stood farther back to admire the whole wall. There was the saddle, properly supported now, a good saddle, not fancy but comfortable. She'd found it at the horse sale two weeks ago. Beside it hung the white stitched bridle, and beside that, in all its glory, hung the silver mounted bridle that would be Clipper's when he grew into it.

She hung the hammer back where it belonged and lifted down Lady Bay's bridle. It was too good a day to stay out of the sunshine one minute longer.

Brown mare and creamy foal were grazing in the front pasture near Karen's barrel-racing barrels. Clipper had to sprawl out his long front legs in order to reach the grass with his teeth; he seemed to be bowing. He took a few bites, then threw his head up and galloped away, in strides that were unbelievably graceful, considering his legs. He was fascinated by the flapping laundry in the adjoining yard, and he alternately stared at it, ran away from it, and ignored it to eat a few more bites of grass.

Lady Bay saw Karen and began moving toward her by slow stages, eating as she came. She was slim and shining and, for now at least, moving soundly. She was not a beautiful horse nor ever would be, but she was kind and honest and she had the unmistakable look of a horse that is loved.

Clipper came, too. He scuttered up to Karen bright-eyed but too playful to hold still for petting today. He nipped at Karen, then leaped behind his mother to peer back around her tail, and challenge Karen to catch him.

"What a brat," Karen said to Lady Bay as she slipped on the bridle. "You should bring him up better."

She climbed onto the mare's back, and reached down to scratch Clipper's bulging forehead. The cream baby fuzz was growing out now, leaving circles of rich gold around his eyes and muzzle. "Gonna be a beauty," she whispered.

Off they went across the pasture, the mare in an easy lope, the girl sitting loose but erect, the foal sweeping in mad circles around his mother.

A truck went by on the road, and honked. Harley's truck. Karen reined in, surprised, and watched as the truck turned into the farm drive. She rode slowly toward the gate, toward the figure who came to lean over it, watching her.

She didn't want to see him.

She was cured of him, and she didn't want to start hurting again.

"Hi there, honey," he called. His hat was pushed back to let the sun come full onto his face. It was the same face she had loved for years. Same eyes, same silvery wavy hair, same big smile.

But something was missing. Karen sat on her horse and looked down into his face, and thought, *He's ordinary.*

"Hello, Harley."

"Haven't seen you for a while, honey. Thought you might be mad at me, or some such."

"No. I'm not mad."

His eyes shifted away from hers, and fixed on Clipper. "That's a mighty good-looking colt you got there. Mighty good-looking. I figured that's what you'd get. See, I knew the mare was bred to a palomino stallion, and I knew she'd thrown palomino colts before, so I figured the chances were good of her having one this time. And you know, palominos are getting scarce anymore. That's going to be a valuable horse. That's why I was charging you the four hundred for the mare. But I didn't want to get your hopes up, in case she wasn't in foal, so I just made up that story about the girl dying and all, because I thought so much of you, and—"

"Harley," Karen said, "stop it."

"Why, what—"

"Just stop telling me lies. I used to be stupid enough to believe you, but I'm not anymore. So you can save those stories for some other dumb kid with a little money saved up."

"Aw, come on, sweetheart, you don't mean—"

"Yes I do, Harley, and quit calling me honey and sweetheart all the time. I don't like it."

For the first time in Karen's memory there was no trace of a smile on Harley's face. "Why, Karen, I thought you was my special little friend."

"I was. But who wants a friend that lies to them all the time. And cheats them."

Harley's face hardened. "Now Karen, I never cheated you. Look what you got for your two hundred dollars." He waved toward Clipper.

But Karen was strong and sure, as she had never been before. "Yes. I ended up getting my money's worth, but in spite of you, not because of you. You sold me a foundered mare that you probably didn't pay more than fifty dollars for, if that much. No," she held up her hand, "I've been around enough by now to have a pretty good idea what you paid for Lady Bay. You told me a cock-and-bull story about her past history, and now you're trying to tell me another one.

"You listen to me, Harley Williams. When I was a little kid I used to dream that you were my daddy, I wanted one so bad, and just worshiped you. So finding out that I didn't mean anything to you, except a chance to make a little money, that really hurt me, Harley. You knew what you were doing to me, and you did it anyway, and I'm not letting you do it again. I really loved you, you know? And that was okay, because I was too young to know what you were really like, so it was understandable. But I do know now. And I'd be stupid to waste my—love—giving it to somebody like you."

She caught her breath, and went on more calmly. "So you're not my friend anymore, Harley, and I hate that, because I miss you. But you don't deserve me."

She reined the mare away and kicked her into a gallop. The pasture was too small to get out of Harley's sight, but she stayed at the far end until he returned to his truck and drove away. It was several minutes before her hands stopped trembling, but when they did, she felt grand.

❈ Fourteen ❈

In a truck stop cafe in southern Wyoming, a big, smiling, silver-haired man leaned on the counter and said to the waitress, "About three thousand acres, more or less. I don't hardly bother to count them. Just finished building me a new ranch house, nice place, logs, you know. Three stone fireplaces, and the biggest ole bearskin rug you ever did see. Chun Lo, that's my cook, he's always tripping over that blamed rug. Cusses it out in Chinese."

The waitress laughed, and he laughed with her, and closed his hands over hers.

ABOUT THE AUTHOR

LYNN HALL was born in Illinois and lives now near Cedar Rapids, Iowa, in a stone cottage that she designed and built primarily by herself. She is the author of many popular books for a wide range of readers, including *The Leaving, A Horse Called Dragon* and other books about Dragon, and *Mystery of Pony Hollow.*

Her hobbies include breeding, riding, and showing Paso Fino horses and breeding and showing English cocker spaniels.